2/5/20

D1246075

For my father,
with love and thanks for his support

MARRY AND BRIGHT

LAURA DURHAM

BROADMOOR BOOKS

CHAPTER 1

"Are you sure this isn't too much?" I asked as I draped a string of white Christmas lights over the top of my living room window.

Kate looked up from where she stood at my wooden dining room table unpacking a box of ivory pillar candles. "Of course it isn't too much, Annabelle. You know what they say, nothing succeeds like excess."

I looked around my apartment, usually the picture of simplicity and less-is-more decor, and wondered if we hadn't taken the concept too far. Glass cylinder vases filled with colorful glass ball ornaments sat in the middle of the coffee table, dining table, and the counter dividing my kitchen and living room. Large paper stars that resembled snowflakes hung from the ceiling at various points so that anyone over five feet tall had to duck and weave to make it across the room, and a red berry wreath hung over the flat screen TV on one wall. A candle that smelled like gingerbread cookies burned in the kitchen, reminding me that I'd only had a bottled Frappuccino and granola bar for breakfast.

"Did Oscar Wilde say that?" I asked, stepping down from the stool.

Kate flipped her blond bob off her face. "I always thought Richard came up with that one. It sounds like him." She held up two pillar candles. "Speaking of too much, remind me again why you have boxes of battery-operated pillar candles."

"From the Hunter wedding," I said. "Remember how they wanted to buy the candles instead of renting them from the florist, but they didn't have anywhere to store ten boxes of candles so they asked me to hang on to them?"

Kate's mouth dropped open. "That wedding was three years ago."

"I know," I said, joining her at the table and flicking the underneath switch on a chunky candle. "That's why I'm conscripting them into service for the holidays. My office is reaching maximum wedding leftovers capacity."

As the owner of the Washington, DC wedding planning company Wedding Belles, I'd inherited everything from pillar candles to leftover cocktail napkins to extra Jordan almonds from nearly seven years' worth of couples. My home office down the hall was filled with boxes of items waiting to be picked up by brides and grooms although most, I knew, never would be. Once the wedding was over, the desire for pastel candies and anything wrapped up in tulle seemed to be abandoned as quickly as the pre-wedding diets.

"I think after three years, the candles are yours," my assistant said. "What other goodies do you have tucked away in the office? I might be in need of some holiday gifts."

I eyed her. "Does this mean I'm getting a pillar candle from you this year?"

"Don't be silly." She arranged candles between the glass cylinders of ornaments that ran down the counter dividing my living room and kitchen. "I was talking about gifts to give the men I'm dating."

"How many gifts are we talking?" Kate's dating life was active, to say the least. "I doubt most men would be thrilled with the kinds of things left over from weddings, unless one of them is dying for a 'Gillian and Ted' wine opener."

"Not many. I was actually looking for something small to give as a token to the men I'm breaking up with, but I wouldn't mind a 'Gillian and Ted' wine opener."

"You're breaking up right before Christmas?" I asked. "And you need consolation prizes?"

"Now you're making me sound heartless." She rested a hand on her hip-hugger jeans. "I've decided to turn over a new leaf and start the year by dating intentionally, which means I need to clear out the men who aren't long-term prospects."

"Dating intentionally? I thought you made it a policy to avoid any relationship longer than the average life span of a goldfish." I placed two candles on the bookshelf by my front door and arranged the small bowl that held my keys between them. "What does 'dating intentionally' even mean? It sounds a little new-agey for you."

"Your relationship with Reese has inspired me," she said. "I admire how you two took it slow, and neither of you lost yourself when you moved in together. Most women vanish once they get a serious boyfriend, but you've still made time for me and for Richard and the rest of the friends you had before Reese came along."

"Thanks," I said, "but it's not like I had a choice. You work for me, so I couldn't exactly stop seeing you, and if I'd ghosted Richard, he would have made a voodoo doll with long auburn hair and used it as a pincushion."

"He wouldn't hex *you*. I wouldn't put it past him to have a voodoo doll that's tall, dark, and hunky like your boyfriend though." Kate smirked at me. "Come to think of it, I wouldn't mind a doll like that."

Even though I'd only moved in with my cop boyfriend, Mike Reese, a couple of months ago, I'd made a concerted effort to spend time with my friends so my best friend, Richard Gerard, wouldn't have any reason to feel left out.

"Speaking of the city's most dramatic caterer, why isn't Richard here helping us decorate your apartment?" Kate asked. "I would have thought he'd relish this since you've never really done much to your place aside from hanging up a sad fake-pine wreath."

"Well, part of the reason I'm going all out for the holidays is to bring us all together," I said. "I thought we should have a party for our crew here to celebrate another successful year."

"And to celebrate surviving another year."

I knew Kate meant the run-ins we'd had with kidnappers, jewel thieves, and murderers while planning weddings for the city's most famous and infamous. "You make it sound like we plan weddings in a war zone."

She shrugged. "There have been days. . ." She flopped onto my yellow twill couch. "So what does a crew party have to do with Richard not being here?"

"If we're having a party, we need a tree, right?" I pointed to a corner I'd cleared out next to one of the tall windows where a tree stand stood at the ready. "Richard and Reese are out getting the Christmas tree."

Kate nearly dropped the candle she was holding. "Are you telling me you sent your boyfriend and best friend out on a team-building exercise? I hope they don't kill each other in the process."

"I made sure Reese didn't take his gun." I liked to think he would never shoot an unarmed man, but after a few hours of Richard nitpicking Fraser firs, I couldn't guarantee it.

"Assuming both Richard and Reese return from this expedition in one piece, a holiday party sounds like fun." Kate rubbed her hands together. "We should do a secret Santa gift exchange. That way we don't go bankrupt buying everyone presents."

"Or so everyone doesn't get identical 'Gillian and Ted' wine openers from you."

"Exactly." She winked at me. "Although you might get a wine opener *and* a candle."

I put a hand to my heart. "I'm touched."

"Will this shindig be before or after the Douglas wedding?"

"Before," I said. "We might not be alive after another Debbie and Darla event, even if it is the son's wedding this time."

Debbie and Darla were a mother-daughter duo we'd first worked with when we'd planned Darla's very WASPy wedding to Turner Grant the Third. The women had rarely been sober for any of our meetings with them, and Darla's wedding had been a bourbon-soaked extravaganza. Even though the son's bride-to-be did not consider mint juleps to be the breath of life like the family she was marrying into did, any party with Debbie and Darla was bound to be eventful.

"Coming through." The door to my apartment flew open, and Richard strode into the room with both arms waving. "Make way, people. Make way."

The tip of a tree poked through the doorway, and then Reese lurched into view, covered almost entirely by the prickly green branches of the pine tree he held with both arms. "Don't worry. I've got it."

Richard pushed the couch over an inch. "Right through here, Detective."

I rushed over and grabbed the sagging trunk of the tree as Reese struggled to keep it from falling to the floor. Bits of pine needles adorned his chocolate-brown hair, and he tried to blow both an errant curl and a branch off his forehead.

"Did you carry this up the entire staircase by yourself?" I asked.

"Don't be ridiculous." Richard touched a hand to his dark hair, still perfectly spiked up. "I navigated and opened all the doors."

"That's true," Reese said. "If it hadn't been for Richard, I never would have known which way to turn at each of the landings."

Richard sniffed. "Well, not all of us dress like lumberjacks. I couldn't afford to get pine sap on my Armani pants."

Kate eyed Reese's jeans, untucked blue flannel shirt, and brown lace-up boots. "Too bad. The lumberjack look is a good look."

Reese and I got the tree across the room and lowered it into the stand. I stood back and admired the full tree that nearly reached the ceiling. I wrapped my arms around my boyfriend as he wiped both sweat and pine needles off his face. "It's perfect."

"Of course it's perfect," Richard said. "It's not too skinny. It's not too fat. It doesn't have any gaps. It doesn't lean to one side. Trust me, we made sure this was the best tree out there."

Reese let out a long breath. "He's right about that. Richard insisted we go to seven different lots before we found this one."

Kate put a hand over her mouth, I presumed to stifle a laugh. "Seven? That must have taken hours."

"Yep." Reese kissed my forehead. "Four to be exact."

"Why don't I get you both a drink?" I suggested, giving Reese a final squeeze and heading for the kitchen.

Richard sank down on the couch next to Kate. "That would be divine. Picking out trees is exhausting."

I opened my refrigerator and looked in the door for where Reese kept the microbrew beers he enjoyed. I picked out two bottles. Richard wasn't usually a fan of beer, but I didn't happen to have a bottle of wine. As I closed the door, I felt an arm reach around me.

"I couldn't wait," Reese said, taking one of the beers from me and enveloping me in a hug. "This was the only thing that kept me from killing Richard for the past four hours."

"The thought of a cold beer?" I turned around and leaned into him, feeling the hard muscles of his chest.

"No, the thought of you. And knowing how unhappy you'd be with me if I came back without your best friend."

I looked up at him. "I'm sorry Richard was so . . . well, so Richard, but thank you for going with him. It means a lot to me, and I think he's really warming up to you."

He twisted off the cap of his beer bottle and took a swig. "Yay me."

"I should probably get this to Richard," I said, holding up the other bottle. "Even if he barely broke a sweat."

As I took a step toward the living room, Reese pulled me back and kissed me. His lips were soft, and I could taste a hint of pale ale as he deepened the kiss. He grinned when he let go and left me blinking up at him. "That's another thing that kept me from becoming homicidal."

I tried to regain my composure as I walked back into the living room and handed Richard a beer.

He looked perplexed. "What is this?"

"Reese's favorite," I said. "He thought you'd appreciate it."

Richard couldn't stop himself from smiling. "Did he now?" He nodded at Reese as the detective came back in and sat down on the overstuffed chair. "Well, never let it be said that Richard Gerard is not up for a little adventure."

"So what do you think of Annabelle's apartment so far?" Kate asked, sweeping an arm wide. "Can you believe all of this was done with leftovers from past weddings?"

"Yes, I can," Richard said as he glanced around the room. "As a matter of fact, just seeing all these things is giving me wedding day flashbacks."

Kate gave him a dismissive wave. "No one else will know, and I think it shows just how creative and clever wedding planners can be."

Richard took a long draw from his beer and grimaced as he swallowed it. He set the bottle on my coffee table and stood. "It's been delightful, but I'd better retrieve my dog from your nutty neighbor before she decides to give him a perm."

"Hermes would look adorable with curly hair," Kate said.

"He would look like a poodle." Richard walked to the door and picked up his crossbody man bag from where he'd left it on the floor. "Yorkies do not have curly hair."

"If Leatrice asks, I'm not here," I said. As fond as I was of my downstairs neighbor, I was not as fond of her habit of popping in unannounced when Reese and I were trying to have some alone time, or when Kate and I were trying to work, or when I was trying to enjoy a few moments of quiet.

"Consider it done." Richard opened the door and paused with his hand on the knob.

Buster and Mack, our favorite florists and good friends, stood in the doorway. The two burly men each topped six feet and three hundred pounds and both sported goatees—one dark red and the other brown. They had bald heads and tattoos that were mostly covered by the black leather pants, vests, and jackets they wore. A "Road Riders for Jesus" patch emblazoned the front of their vests, as well as one that said "Ride Hard Die Saved."

My eyes dropped to the squirming bundle in Mack's arms that wore a pink-and-blue-striped cap and was wrapped in a pink blanket.

"Is that a . . ." Kate began.

"Baby?" I finished for her when I finally found my voice.

Richard turned around, his eyes wide. "Does anyone else feel like one of these things just doesn't belong?"

"We didn't know where else to come," Buster said, his deep voice cracking. "You've got to help us."

CHAPTER 2

"*W*hy do you have a baby?" I said as the two men came inside.

"Is there something you want to tell us?" Richard asked, taking a step back from the now-whimpering infant. Richard was not a fan of anything as unpredictable and messy as a baby.

Mack jiggled the tiny baby, and she quieted. Sleeping in the crook of his beefy arm must have been like being nestled in a warm cocoon. He looked down at her, his face pinched. "Someone left her on our doorstep."

Kate scooted over and patted the cushion next to her for Mack to sit. "At Lush? Why would someone leave a baby outside a floral shop?"

"Not Lush," Buster said. "At the Born Again Biker Church."

"Oh." Kate nodded. "That makes more sense."

Richard cocked an eyebrow. "Does it?"

Buster and Mack were part of a Christian motorcycle gang, and even though I'd never been inside, I knew their church was in a nondescript building in the warehouse district of Northeast DC where there was plenty of parking for Harleys, and no one lived

9

nearby to care about the sound of revving motors on a Sunday morning. Their gang consisted of bikers like them with piercings, tattoos, and questionable pasts. Many were former members of what they called 1 percent gangs, the violent criminal organizations like the Hell's Angels and Bandidos, who had seen the error of their ways and now tried to help other lost souls.

Mack sat down on the sofa, and the springs groaned under his weight. "We were cleaning up after our service. Buster and I are serving as ushers this month. Nearly everyone else had cleared out, and we were locking up when we saw her."

"You didn't see anyone close to the building when you found her?" Reese asked. "Sometimes people who leave babies stick around to make sure they're found."

Buster shook his head. "No, but to tell you the truth, we were so startled we could have missed seeing someone."

"I can imagine." I walked behind Mack and leaned over his shoulder to get a better look at the sleeping child. I wasn't an expert on babies, but this one looked to be only a few weeks old. Her tiny face was round and plump, and she had a wisp of light-brown hair peeking out below her knit cap. One pink fist was in her mouth, and she appeared to be sucking on it.

Buster swung a pale-green quilted diaper bag down from his shoulder and let it flop to the floor. "She came with this and a note." He dug a piece of paper out of the side pocket of the bag and handed it to Reese.

I joined Reese as he went to the dining room table holding the note by the top corner and two fingers. He put the crumpled sheet of lined notebook paper on the flat surface and we both leaned over it.

"Read it out loud," Kate said.

"I'm sorry." I read from the paper. "Please take care of her. I can't. I only want what is best for Merry, and it isn't me."

"That's so sad." Kate put a hand to her mouth. "She even has a name."

"Merry," I said. "As in Merry Christmas."

"That's a little on the nose, wouldn't you say?" Richard asked. "A baby found in December named Merry. Are we sure there isn't a hidden camera somewhere?"

The baby began crying, and Mack started humming—a sound like a throaty rumble that reminded me of his Harley starting up. "You're okay now, little Merry."

Richard cleared his throat. "This is all very sad, but what are you going to do? It's not like you two can take care of her."

"For once, I agree with Richard," Reese said, looking up from examining the note. "We need to call social services."

Mack looked up, his face stormy. "No. I was a foster kid, and I wouldn't wish that on anyone, especially not a sweet little baby."

I didn't know much about either member of my go-to floral team's past, aside from the fact that they'd been designers in New York before coming to DC. Looking at the determined expression on Mack's face, I knew now they'd had experiences I might never understand.

Buster nodded. "Someone left her with us for a reason."

I wondered what kind of person would leave a baby on the threshold of a biker church since DC had safe haven laws that allowed parents to drop off a baby at any hospital anonymously. Either someone desperate who couldn't get to a hospital, didn't know the law, or had a connection to the church.

Mack rocked the baby back and forth, his face softening as he gazed down at her. "That's why we came to you. Whoever left this baby was in a bad place. We need to find them and help them."

"You want us to help you find out who abandoned the baby?" I looked back at the note on the table. "And this note is all we have to go on?"

"You found Kate when she was missing," Buster said. "And you've tracked down more than one killer."

I noticed Reese folding his arms across his chest. "Technically the police discovered the perpetrators. We only helped out."

"A habit I'm trying to break her of," Reese said. "You really should turn this matter over to the police. Our department has more resources than any civilian could access."

Buster and Mack were silent.

Kate stood up. "I think we all need something to drink." She looped her arm through mine and pulled me toward the kitchen. "I know I do."

Once we'd ducked into the kitchen, I opened the refrigerator door. "A few more mircrobrews and a few Diet Dr Peppers. Oh, and one last bottled Mocha Frappuccino."

Kate peered over my shoulder. "I can tell Richard hasn't been here for a while. He always kept you stocked up with bubbly and wine." She motioned to the beers. "Let's bring those. We need to lower the temperature in the room a bit."

"Buster and Mack don't drink," I said.

She made a face. "I've got to tell you, that's the only thing about them that makes me wary."

I grabbed two bottles by the neck and gave her a look. "Really? *That's* what makes you wary?"

She reached around me and took two cans of soda from the door. "Well, that and the fact that they don't curse. How they can work with brides and not want to drop the F-bomb every ten minutes is beyond me."

I lowered my voice in case they could hear me through the open space above the dividing counter between the rooms. "What do you think about this baby thing?"

"Pretty grateful no one dropped a baby on my doorstep, I can tell you that much."

I looked at Kate in her low-slung jeans and crop sweater. Kate embraced being single with a vigor usually reserved for religious zealots, and I had a hard time imagining her settling down, much less wanting to be a mother.

Kate nudged the refrigerator door closed with her hip. "That being said, they are our friends and they asked for our help. If the holidays aren't the time for helping out friends in need, I don't know when is."

I followed her back into the living room feeling properly chagrined for hesitating about helping Buster and Mack. Kate was right. Our friends were trying to do a good thing. Helping them find who left the baby was the least we could do.

Kate handed Buster and Mack each a can of Diet Dr Pepper and took one of the beer bottles from me, twisting off the cap and taking a sip. "So has Reese agreed to help us yet?"

My boyfriend shook his head. "No way am I getting roped into another one of your crazy plans."

Kate took her place on the couch again, tucking her legs up under her. "Crazy seems like a strong word."

"I don't blame you, Detective," Richard said, nodding his head at Reese. "This isn't a case of trying to find a killer before they find us or trying to find Kate before the kidnapper eliminates her. If someone left a baby for a bunch of bikers to find, they aren't winning any parent-of-the-year contests. This child is better off being put into the system so a good home can be found for her."

Mack sucked in air and Buster growled. Richard moved closer to Reese.

"I think both sides make good points," I said. "Since Buster and Mack found the child, I think we should at least attempt to do what they're asking. If we can't find the person who left the baby after a week, maybe they can consider letting her be put up for adoption."

A look passed between the two men and both gave curt nods.

"That seems fair," Buster said.

"So do you have room at your place for a baby?" Kate asked.

"We already put out a call to our biker brotherhood." Mack shifted the baby to his other arm. "Slim and Big Beard are bringing us a bassinet and some secondhand baby clothes tonight."

"What about car seats and swings and changing tables?" Kate took a swig from her beer. "Wait a second. Do they make infant car seats for Harleys?"

Mack laughed. "We're using one of the floral vans instead of our bikes, and she was dropped off in a baby car seat you hook in to the seat belts."

"If you want, I can take a look at it to make sure it's hooked in properly," Reese said. "The police check infant car seats for parents all the time."

Buster let out a breath. "Would you? It took us forever to get it in, and I'm not sure it's right."

"No problem. Where's your van?"

Mack glanced at my wall clock. "We can't do it now. We have to go to the final meeting with Debbie and Darla and the bride-to-be."

Kate looked at me, her eyes bugged out. "I totally forgot about that meeting. We're supposed to be at Lush in ten minutes."

"I lost track of time," I admitted. "This day has flown by."

Kate set her beer on the coffee table and stood up. "We'd better run if we want to beat the client there." She stared down at the sleeping baby. "What are you going to do with her?"

Mack looked at Reese and Richard. "Is there any way one of you could watch her? It would only be for a few minutes. We'll rush right back."

"She'll probably sleep the whole time," Buster added.

Richard staggered back a few steps, his palm pressed to his chest. "You must be out of your mind. I do not do babies."

Mack stood up and walked toward Reese, who also took a step back. "We don't have anyone else to ask."

For once in my life, I felt lucky to have a meeting with a bride.

Richard began to head toward the door, and Reese caught him by the sleeve. "Don't even think about leaving me alone with this."

"What?" Richard spluttered. "If you think I . . ."

"Oh, I do think you're going to stay right here." Reese grinned showing lots of teeth. "I'd hate to think of what might happen to you if you don't. APBs on all your catering trucks, speed cameras installed on every corner of your neighborhood, a certain BMW convertible booted every single morning."

Richard gasped. "You wouldn't."

Reese looked at the baby then back at Richard. "Try me."

Richard mumbled something about police brutality before shrugging off his jacket and hanging it over the back of a dining room chair. "It appears I'll be staying."

Mack transferred the baby into Reese's arms and touched her cheek gently. "Thank you, Detective."

Richard cleared his throat.

"Thank you, too, Richard," I said, scooping up my purse and backing out the door with Kate. "We'll be back before you know it."

Buster and Mack reluctantly walked out into the hallway, glancing back at the two men and the baby.

Reese winked at me as he swayed Merry back and forth. "Don't worry. Uncle Reese and Auntie Richard have this under control."

The last thing I saw before pulling the door closed was Richard's face as he shot daggers at my grinning boyfriend. "Auntie Richard indeed!"

CHAPTER 3

"*S*o how can we make this the quickest floral meeting in history?" Kate asked as we followed Buster and Mack into their chic Georgetown shop.

I breathed in a combination of fresh flowers and dark roast coffee, and my eyes went from the galvanized metal buckets of roses and hydrangea stacked on shelves along one wall to the shiny-chrome cappuccino maker dominating a high metal table at the back of the shop. "Hope the clients are a no-show?"

"We do not want that." Buster's boots echoed off the cement floor as he strode to the back of the space and fired up the high-end coffee machine. "I'm already cutting it close with any changes to the floral order. They do know this isn't a meeting to rethink the look, don't they?"

"I explained it to Darla." I hopped up onto a stool around a high top table. "I can't guarantee she was sober when I told her though."

"I can bet she wasn't," Kate said.

I looked out the glass front of the store and could see shoppers

16

and tourists walking by. No sign of our clients. Then again, we had made it across Georgetown in record time. I reached into my black Longchamp bag and pulled out the file for the Douglas wedding, setting it in front of me and flipping to the latest version of the floral proposal. "You'll send me a new proposal after today, right?"

Mack produced a box of cookies from a cabinet and began arranging them on a plate. "If there are changes."

"So that's a yes," Kate said, taking the seat next to me.

I turned to the back of the proposal, took a pen out of my bag, and clicked it. "If we're going to figure out who left that baby, I need to get more details."

Mack joined us and put the cookies in the middle of the table. "Ask us anything."

"Are those chocolate chip?" Kate asked, eyeing the oversized cookies. "You're not trying to sneak a raisin by me, are you?"

Mack winked at her. "Never. Those are made with real butter, real sugar, and lots of real chocolate."

The steamer nozzle hissed behind us as Buster put the finishing touches on four cappuccinos before carrying them over to us on a sleek metal tray. "There isn't much to tell aside from what we told you earlier. We searched the diaper bag, but the only thing in it of any interest was the note."

Kate took her cappuccino, putting her nose close to the surface and inhaling deeply. "Between the cookies and the gourmet coffee, I may never leave."

I tapped my pen on the table and let my own cup cool in front of me. "I'm assuming none of your members or church attendees were pregnant before today."

"Most of the people who come to the Born Again Biker Church are men, though we do get some wives and lady bikers. None of them have been pregnant that I've noticed," Mack said.

"Nope," Buster backed him up. "And even of the guys with girl-friends, I can't think of a one who's mentioned a pregnancy. Of course, we'll ask everyone."

I made a note that the church didn't have any expectant mothers. "So that's a bit of a dead end. What about homeless women? Any of those hang around the church?"

Mack leaned forward on his elbows and steepled his hands in front of his face. "Northeast DC has its share of homeless people, but not too many women, and none of them in our neighborhood young enough to have a baby."

Strike two. I made a note on my paper.

"What else is in that area?" Kate asked, taking a sip of her coffee. "Maybe the person was there for another reason and saw the church."

"Good thinking," I said, motioning to her to wipe the trace of foam off her upper lip. "What other businesses are near the church?"

"Aside from the Atlas Performing Arts Center not too far away, we've had a real influx of trendy restaurants lately," Buster said, taking a large gulp of his cappuccino. "We have a Bullfrog Bagels, Toki Underground, and even a dumpling shop and cock-tail bar that stays open until two a.m."

Kate's eyes lit up. "I need to check out the H Street Corridor again. First Union Market takes off and now this."

"I'm surprised you aren't up on it," I said. "Considering how much you go out."

She sighed. "I've had a string of politicos lately who don't want to leave Capitol Hill. See? This is exactly what I was talking about earlier. It's time for me to clean house and shake things up a bit. Date some men who like adventure."

"I thought you wanted to turn over a new leaf and stop dating so many men."

"That was before I found out about the dumpling and cocktail bar," she said.

I shook my head as I turned my attention back to my list. "So theoretically anyone going to those places could have seen your church and gotten the idea to drop off the baby."

Buster rubbed a hand over his dark-brown goatee. "Since our church isn't usually open at night, I would think it would be someone who sees the neighborhood in the daylight."

"So maybe an employee instead of a patron," I said then shook my head. "That's still an awful lot of people to consider."

"And no idea where to start," Kate said.

"I still think Annabelle was right earlier." Mack shifted on his stool, and both his leather pants and the stool legs groaned. "It has to be someone with a connection to our church or someone in it. They had to feel like it was a safe place to leave the baby. The note wasn't written by someone who didn't care what happened to Merry."

I agreed with him. The person who had written that sad note had thought they were doing the best for their child.

A bell above the door rang as it was flung open, and Darla and Debbie bustled inside along with a blast of cold air and a willowy woman with long white-blond hair.

"So sorry we're late," Darla said, walking in front of the two younger women. "We were having a late lunch at that new Peruvian Gastrobar."

Debbie, almost an exact replica of her mother from the brown bobs held back with Burberry headbands to the red Tory Burch shoes, winked at us. "We're on a pisco sour kick."

I braced myself for the possibility they would want to change the entire theme of the wedding around their new favorite cocktail. With Debbie and Darla, anything was possible.

"Hi, Caroline," I said to the woman I assumed was the bride-to-be. "How was your flight from Los Angeles?"

"It was fine," she said, rubbing her arms briskly. "I just didn't think it would be so cold."

Darla laughed. "California girls have such thin blood."

I knew the bride was a California girl, but it seemed odd that she didn't think DC would be cold in December. To be fair, I only knew her through the emails we'd exchanged, and most of her replies to my questions had been efficiently brief.

In addition to the almost blindingly blond hair, Caroline seemed as opposite from her future in-laws as you could be. She wore black from head to toe, and her only makeup seemed to be dark eyeliner and red lipstick. If I didn't know better, I would have called her style goth glam.

How had we missed this? Since Daniel Douglas and his fiancee lived on the other side of the country, we'd done all the planning with Debbie and Darla. I felt a flutter of panic as I realized that nothing about the wedding we'd planned reflected the bride in front of me.

Darla threw an arm around Caroline. "She's tickled about all the wonderful ideas we've come up with, aren't you honey?"

Caroline gave me a smile that didn't meet her heavily lined eyes. "Tickled."

Oh boy.

"Let me get you all some cappuccinos so you can warm up." Buster hurried to his coffee station. "It's gotten bitterly cold out there."

Caroline pulled her coat tighter around her neck as she took a seat next to me at the high table. "This is why I hate winter."

Kate shot me a look, and I knew she was thinking the same thing. Why on earth was this woman having a December wedding?

It took Debbie two tries to make it onto one of the metal barstools, and Kate had to grab her arm to keep her from tipping over to the other side. Darla leaned against the table, and I got a whiff of expensive perfume and booze. Knowing Darla, she could be wearing the pisco sours as well as drinking them. I wouldn't put it past her to dab top shelf liquor onto her wrists and behind her ears after a spritz of Chanel.

Mack pulled out his copy of the last floral proposal as I flipped mine back over. "Did you have any particular changes in mind, or should we just review the quantities?"

"I wanted to change the bridal bouquet," Caroline said before Darla or Debbie could open their mouths.

"That's a great place to start," Mack said, finding the description of the bouquet on the first page of the proposal. "What part did you want to tweak?"

The bride folded her hands on the table. "I'd like to take out the ivy and berries."

Buster set three steaming hot cappuccinos on the table, and Darla gave the coffees a sad look. "You don't have anything to make these Irish, do you?"

I leaned back and shook my head so that Buster could see me but Debbie and Darla could not.

Buster patted Darla's hand. "I'm so sorry."

Mack glanced down at the proposal and blinked a few times. "You don't like ivy and berries?"

Caroline shuddered. "Too Christmasy."

"But the entire theme of the wedding is holiday inspired," Buster said as he took the seat next to Mack.

Caroline made a face. "I know. I should have looked over things sooner, but work has been insane. I'd really rather the wedding not have anything to do with the holidays."

Darla sucked in her breath. "Does that mean you don't want the Dickens-style carolers for cocktail hour?"

"You're joking, right?" the bride asked.

Darla's cheeks reddened, but I put my hand over hers before she could reply. "It's not the end of the world to cancel the carolers. We can keep it classic with a string quartet."

"I'd rather play some acid jazz from my iPod playlist," Caroline said.

Debbie almost slipped off the stool. "Acid jazz?"

"No problem," I said. "Just send me that playlist, and I'll find a jazz group that can play it."

Mack scribbled in the proposal. "So if we remove the ivy and berries, the bouquets are just roses and mini callas."

"But not the roses and not the white mini callas," Caroline said. "Can you get the ones that are dark purple?"

Mack didn't look up. "Just dark purple mini callas?"

"Caroline, honey," Darla said, taking a sip of her nonalcoholic cappuccino and cringing. "You can't have your girls walking down the aisle with black flowers."

"They're not black," Caroline said. "They're dark purple."

"To-may-to, to-mah-to," Darla said to me in a stage whisper.

"I have no doubt Buster and Mack will come up with something stunning," I said, partly to appease the bride and partly to quiet the mother of the groom. Even though Darla was technically my client and was writing all the checks, I couldn't in good conscience let the bride be steamrolled into a wedding she hated. "Why don't we compromise and have the ceremony feature the dark callas and keep the more seasonal floral designs we've already planned for the reception?"

"I was hoping to have succulents instead of flowers in the middle of the tables," Caroline said.

Nothing said love like a bunch of cactus, I thought as I noticed Darla pale.

"Succulents?" Buster asked. "Why didn't you say succulents in the first place? We've been on such a succulent kick lately."

Mack bobbed his head up and down. "It's true."

"Instead of cactus centerpieces, what about a baby succulent at the top of every guests' place?" I said to Caroline. "Do you like that idea?"

"That could work," Caroline said.

Kate leaned close to Darla. "You know tequila comes from a succulent."

Darla's eyes widened. "You don't say? Maybe we should add a tequila bar to the wedding."

"I think we're good with two gin-and-tonic stations as well as two main bars already," I said. I did not want a rehash of the wedding we'd done where we'd had a tequila fountain instead of a champagne fountain and guests had had to be carried out.

"If you say so," Debbie said. "But I do love a good margarita."

I felt my phone buzz and slipped it out of my pants pocket without looking down. "So are we all set for changes then?"

All three women nodded as they stood and gathered their things, but Caroline pulled me close as her future mother-in-law and sister-in-law teetered off ahead. "I'm telling you now, if I see so much as one holly berry or scrap of velvet ribbon at my wedding, I will walk out."

I opened my mouth to respond, but she released my arm and strode off, the only one of the three who looked like she wasn't about to topple over.

"She's not what I expected," Kate said once the bride was on the sidewalk.

"You didn't expect a blond version of the Grinch?" Buster asked.

Mack threw his pen on the table. "I'm going to have to do an entirely new floral order and have it rushed. The only good thing is no one else will be buying up all the cacti in December."

I looked down at my phone display. "This isn't good."

"I think disaster is the word you're looking for," Buster said.

"What?" Kate asked, noticing my expression and looking over my shoulder.

"It's from Richard," I said, reading from the screen, "SOS. Bring diapers."

Kate put an hand on my shoulder. "I think you may need to move, Annabelle."

CHAPTER 4

"We came as quickly as we could," I said as I pushed open the door to my apartment, a plastic grocery bag filled with diapers swinging from my wrist. "After a quick stop for supplies."

Buster and Mack hurried past me holding their own grocery bags, but stopped a few feet inside to take in the scene in my apartment.

"It's worse than we imagined," Kate whispered, coming up behind me.

I wasn't sure if it was worse, but it was definitely stranger.

Reese stood in the middle of the living room wearing nothing but his jeans, holding the baby—no longer wrapped in a blanket—to his chest. My downstairs neighbor Leatrice was perched on the edge of the couch strumming a ukulele and humming what sounded like the theme to *Hawaii Five-O*. Her sweater had a giant reindeer face and a light-up red nose blinking off and on, which went well with the antler headband holding back her jet-black, flipped-up hair.

I could see Richard's head through the opening between my

living room and kitchen and could tell he stood at the stove. What on earth was he cooking at a time like this? It smelled like he was curdling cream.

Reese's shoulders relaxed when he saw us. "You're back."

Buster and Mack clustered around Reese as they inspected the sleeping baby. She had on nothing but a tiny diaper and was splayed across Reese's chest as he swayed from side to side.

I dropped my bag of disposable diapers on the floor. "Is everything okay? Richard's text sounded panicked."

Reese raised one eyebrow. "Well it would, wouldn't it? It is Richard after all."

"What's going on?" I asked, taking off my coat as I realized my heater was going full blast. "Why are you half naked?"

"Leave the man alone," Kate said as she looked my boyfriend up and down, smiling and nodding. "He clearly had a reason for embracing his inner caveman, and I, for one, think we should encourage it."

I elbowed her, and she yelped.

Leatrice stopped strumming her ukulele and popped up. "Skin-to-skin contact calms the baby. We tried a lot of other things before this finally worked."

"A lot," Reese said, his left eye twitching as he spoke.

"When did you get here?" I asked Leatrice. "I thought you were babysitting Hermes."

"I was, but Richard texted me to come up and help." She looked around the floor. "Hermes is here somewhere." She cupped a hand over her mouth. "He might be pouting. He's a little jealous of the baby."

The baby whimpered, and Leatrice quickly strummed a chord. "She doesn't like it when I stop." She sat back down on the couch and resumed her slow, plodding version of *Hawaii Five-O*, the chords only slightly connected to the melody.

"I didn't know she played the ukulele," Kate said.

I rubbed my temples. "I don't think she does."

"In here," Richard called out in a loud whisper from the kitchen and waved a wooden spoon.

"I'll be right back," I told Reese as I headed to my kitchen.

Richard stood at the stove wearing a Santa apron—a gift from Leatrice I thought I'd hidden well in the back of a drawer—and stirring something in a copper double boiler, while Hermes was curled in the corner with his back to him. The Yorkie's tiny black-and-brown ears were tilted back, so he could listen to what was going on even if he was pretending to ignore it.

I put a hand over my nose. "Is this really the time to be cooking? And what in heaven's name is that? It smells like curdled milk."

Richard put a hand on his hip. "I'll have you know I'm heating up formula."

"In a double boiler? I didn't even know I had a double boiler."

Richard narrowed his eyes at me. "I gave it to you two Christmases ago." He waved a hand at the shiny pot with two handles. "It's top-of-the-line copper and an excellent heat conductor."

"That doesn't explain why you're warming up formula in it," I said, stepping closer and getting a stronger whiff of the strange smell. "I thought you were supposed to put the bottle in a pan of boiling water."

Richard glanced at the double boiler, then looked at me, then looked back at the bubbling formula. "Well how was I supposed to know that? I've never taken care of a baby before. All I know is that your boyfriend asked me to warm up the formula."

I leaned over the simmering contents and noticed a skin forming on top. "How long have you been boiling it?"

"About fifteen minutes. It has to be sterilized, darling," Richard said, giving me an exasperated look.

"The bottles need to be sterilized, Richard. Not the formula itself." I put a hand over my mouth to keep from laughing.

Richard stared down at the bubbling formula. "Oh. I take it we can't give this to the little crying machine?"

I put a hand on his arm. "Probably not."

"Well, that's just great." Richard threw his spoon on the stovetop, and drops of formula splattered onto the counter. "Not only did I spend the last hour listening to a wailing child and a crazy old woman singing television theme songs, but my dog isn't speaking to me and my dish is ruined."

I squeezed his arm. "I think it's very sweet you tried to make her formula."

Richard crossed his arms and turned away. I couldn't help noticing how similar he and Hermes looked as they both faced the wall and pouted.

"If it makes you feel better," I said, "I think Buster and Mack will be taking Merry with them."

Richard twisted around, his mouth turning up at the corners. "They will? Are they all leaving now?" He pushed past me. "Well, I'd better say goodbye to the little angel."

I bent down. "Come on Hermes. I know you're listening to every word I say, and I'm pretty sure you understand me." His head turned toward me ever so slightly. "The baby is leaving."

He jumped up, gave a small yip, and scampered past me, his jeweled collar jingling as he ran.

I followed Richard and Hermes back into the living room and tried not to gape or scream. Not only was Reese shirtless, so were Buster and Mack.

"What happened?" I asked Kate, sidling up to her. "I was only in the kitchen for a few minutes."

"I can't really say." Kate looked shell-shocked. "It all happened so fast."

I'd never seen the biker florists without several layers of leather, and I'd never imagined them being so hairy, especially since neither had a hair on their heads. "I don't suppose those are sweaters?"

Kate shook her head with her lips pressed together. "I'm afraid not."

The men appeared to be taking turns holding the baby to their skin as Leatrice played the theme to *The Love Boat* and sang the words in a high-pitched, off-key warble. I noticed that Reese had stepped away and reached for his blue flannel shirt.

He walked over to me as he slipped it on and began buttoning it. "I hope your meeting went well." I caught the subtext loud and clear. I owed him big time.

"It did," I said. "I mean, the bride changed the entire wedding and threatened to walk out if it is even remotely holiday themed, but aside from that it was great."

He gave me a confused look.

"Thank you again for everything today." I slipped a hand inside his shirt and around his waist. "And thank you for not killing Richard several times over."

He kissed the top of my head and pulled me close. "You're very welcome. It might be one of my greatest achievements to date."

I swatted at him. "Was he that bad?"

"I'll give him credit for trying, but he's really never been within fifty feet of a baby, has he?" Reese laughed. "Once we convinced him you could not swaddle a baby like you fold a pocket square and sent him to the kitchen, things were much smoother."

"Did I hear my name?" Richard joined us, his black leather body bag slung across his chest and Hermes sitting happily inside, his eyes barely peeking above the flap.

"I was just saying how you and I were partners in crime today," Reese said, thumping Richard on the back and sending him forward a few feet.

Richard steadied himself and straightened his shoulders. "I always say it's about teamwork."

I'd never heard Richard say anything close to that, but I chose not to point it out.

"Well, I'd better hit the road," Kate said, glancing at the clock on my wall. "I have a hot date tonight, and I'm going to try to get him to take me somewhere near the H Street Corridor."

"Any particular reason?" Reese asked. Until the past few years, Northeast DC wasn't someplace you actively sought out for great restaurants.

"We were brainstorming people who might have had a reason to leave their baby at the Born Again Biker Church, and we thought that maybe it was someone who worked at one of the new restaurants in the area."

Richard rolled his eyes. "Don't tell me you're getting mixed up in another investigation."

"Yes," Reese said looking down at me. "Please don't tell me."

"This is hardly an investigation," I said. "It's not like there's a crime or a victim or any danger involved."

"All those are debatable," Reese muttered.

Kate hiked her black-and-white-striped Kate Spade purse over her shoulder. "Compared to all the murder investigations we've poked our noses into, this is a cakewalk."

I shot her a look. "Thanks."

"Give me one good reason for trying to track down the person who abandoned this baby," Richard said.

I shrugged. "If you're fine with babysitting, we won't bother."

Richard's face went slack. "What do you mean?"

I cast a glance behind me at the two burly, shirtless men cooing at the baby. "If you think they're going to give up this child, then you haven't been paying attention. If we don't locate the parents, we're all going to be spending a lot more time with baby Merry."

"Count me in," Richard said. "I'm up for whatever it takes to find out who this baby belongs to."

Hermes yipped. Clearly he didn't like sharing the spotlight with anything that was cute and demanding, either.

Reese pinched the bridge of his nose. "I still say this should go through social services." His eyes rested on the baby, and he blinked a few times in quick succession. "But I've also seen how broken the foster system is, and I don't like the thought of her going into that."

Kate nudged me. "Mr. Law and Order is actually a big softie."

"If there isn't any more life-changing drama for today," Richard said, opening my door and pointing a finger at me and Kate, "I'll see you both tomorrow at the OWP holiday party."

I smacked a hand to my forehead. I signed us up for the Organization of Wedding Planners holiday party so long ago it had slipped my mind that it was this week. "I forgot all about that. Wait, why are you going?"

"I got roped into catering it, remember?" He gave me a pointed look, and I felt my face warm as it dawned on me that I'd been the one to do the roping. "Don't worry, darlings, after today a room filled with inebriated wedding planners will be nothing."

Kate and I exchanged a look. Somehow I doubted that.

CHAPTER 5

The glass elevator pinged open, and Kate and I stepped out in front of the National Cathedral. The massive Gothic building rose above us with its three main towers jutting pointed spires over three hundred feet into the air. The main entrance held three arched doorways adorned with intricate stone carvings and a stained glass rose window above the central arch.

Even though I couldn't see them from my vantage point, I knew the cathedral boasted gargoyles in the image of bishops, yuppies, and even Darth Vader. Flying buttresses extended off the sides like carved stone tent poles securing the sanctuary to the ground. The cathedral's ivory limestone reflected the light and made the building almost blinding in the midday sun, its silhouette stark against the clear blue sky.

Kate slipped on her oversized sunglasses while I raised a hand to shield my eyes as I pulled my green angora scarf closer to my neck. It was sunny but cold, with a biting wind whipping down the long stretch of Wisconsin Avenue and making me shiver.

"I can't get used to the idea of having parties inside a church,"

Kate said as we followed the sidewalk past some bare-limbed trees.

I grasped the handrail as we went up the short flight of steps leading to the front door. "Correction, a cathedral."

"Either way," Kate said, "it feels odd to get soused at church."

I glanced at my wrist even though I wore no watch. "Who says we're going to get soused? It's lunchtime."

The glass double doors stood open, and a pair of women smiled at us from inside the church foyer. Kate lowered her voice. "It's still a holiday party. You know how those get."

We stepped inside and said hello to the greeters who directed us to a table with name tags in the shape of wreaths. I unwrapped my scarf and attached the name tag to my red-and-black-plaid dress, feeling grateful the tags used magnets instead of pins that leave holes in fabric.

"Speaking of cocktails, how was your date?" I asked her. "Did you hit the H Street Corridor?"

"We ended up at the oyster bar in Union Market, but it's not too far from H Street." She picked up the wreath name tag with her name on it. "I have to tell you, Annabelle, there are so many new restaurants and businesses in northeast, it would be nearly impossible to sift through all the employees."

That's what I'd been afraid of. "Thanks for checking it out."

"You know me," she said. "It's always work, work, work."

Kate took off her coat, and I blinked a few times. "So you have an issue with drinking in church but not with wearing a micromini?"

Kate tugged the hemline of the red dress which was tight at her waist and flared out. "I wouldn't say micro."

I eyed the skirt which rested several inches above mid-thigh. "It barely covers your—"

"Hoo-boy!" Fern, our go-to wedding day hairstylist, rushed up to us. "I'm glad you two are here."

He took our coats and waved for us to follow him to the coat check station off to one side, handing us a claim ticket once he'd passed the coats to the tuxedoed attendant.

With his arms free, I was finally able to take in his outfit. Covered from head to toe in forest-green velvet, Fern wore both pants and a cropped jacket that were tapered and slim fitting. He'd tied a white silk ascot at his throat and pinned it with a garnet the size of a small egg, and he'd pulled his dark hair back in a low ponytail that barely dipped below his collar. Nothing about this ensemble surprised me since Fern considered dressing to the season and occasion the height of creative expression. I was just happy he hadn't dressed in bishop's robes.

"Why are you at an Organization of Wedding Planners party?" I asked, returning the air kiss he gave me. "Not that I'm not thrilled to see you."

Kate looped an arm though his. "He's my plus one."

Why hadn't I thought to bring a plus one? Not that I'd want to subject anyone not in the wedding industry to the experience.

We walked from the foyer into the sanctuary, and I paused for a moment. The wooden chairs that usually sat in rows and filled the long sanctuary were gone, replaced by an elevated, round DJ booth in the center, and both cocktail tables and food stations fanned out around it. Patterned green lighting had been projected up the stone columns and vaulted ceiling, giving the cavernous space an otherworldly feel.

Kate and I had coordinated several wedding ceremonies at the National Cathedral, each one with masses of traditional white flowers on the altar and a bride processing to sacred music. The rules for weddings at the cathedral were quite strict, and the vergers who ran the show carried long ceremonial staffs for pomp and enforcement (or so it always felt to me). It was strange to see the religious space decked out like a nightclub.

"Have you seen Richard?" I asked Fern as my eyes scanned the people mingling around tables draped in shimmering red cloths.

"He was by the poke' station earlier." Fern motioned to a long wooden table to the right topped with glass bowls.

"Poke'?" Kate asked. "That's the Hawaiian version of ceviche, right?"

I nodded as I looked for Richard around the busy station. "Raw fish, yes."

"I wonder how he's making that fit in with the holiday theme."

"Have you tried the smoked scallops, ladies?" Bambie Sitwell, or Boob Job Bambie as we called her, asked as she walked up to us. "They're literally smoking them at that table over there."

I glanced at the square table where a chef in a white jacket appeared to be placing small plates of scallops under smoke-filled glass domes. "Hi, Bambie. Are they good?"

She closed her heavily made-up eyes for a moment and brushed a strand of hair off her Botoxed forehead. "Divine." Her eyes popped open. "But not as addictive as these mistletoe margaritas." She held up a large glass coupe filled with lime-green liquid and garnished with a green sprig of what I could only assume was mistletoe.

Kate's head swiveled around. "Did you say margarita?"

Bambie waved a hand laden with rings toward a bar that appeared to be draped in ivy and red berries. Kate and Fern took off in that direction without a backward glance.

Great. Now I was stuck talking with Boob Job Bambie, whose only topic of conversation seemed to be her latest trip to the med spa or her latest well-heeled, long-in-the-tooth husband. And was Richard really serving tequila at noon inside a cathedral? I knew he was what he considered a lapsed Catholic, and the National Cathedral was an Episcopal church, but this seemed a bit sacrilegious even for him.

I looked past Barbie's teased blond helmet and spotted my best friend's dark, spiky hair above the crowd. I caught his eye as he came into view ,and a look of relief passed over his face.

He rushed over and gave me a perfunctory hug, ignoring Bambie who didn't seem to notice as she floated off to talk to someone else. "You got here just in time."

"Why?" I asked.

He straightened his dove-gray tie layered on his dark-gray shirt. "I was desperate for some intelligent conversation, that's why. All the planners want to talk about is 'the list'." He made air quotes with his fingers.

"You mean the *Capital Weddings Magazine* list? Is that out yet?"

Capital Weddings Magazine published a list in their January issue of the top wedding vendors as voted on by the DC wedding industry. The issue was one of their best sellers, and brides-to-be and their mothers had been known to use the list as a bible. Making the magazine was a boost to business, and getting the coveted starred listing as the top vote getter was the jewel in any wedding professional's crown.

"Rumor has it early issues have just come off the presses, and an issue is floating around the party somewhere," Richard said, looking nonplussed. It was easy for him to be so nonchalant since his company, Richard Gerard Catering, had been a fixture on the list since it began, and he'd gotten the star next to his name more than once.

"Don't you want to get a peek at it?" I asked him, peering around and trying to spot someone flashing a bridal magazine.

"I suppose, but it's not like the list changes dramatically from year to year." Richard studied a passing waiter then nodded approvingly.

"We only made it onto the list two years ago," I said. "I just hope we don't fall off after all the . . ."

"Murders?" Fern asked as he and Kate joined us, each holding a bright-green margarita. "You didn't. I checked."

I put a hand to my heart. "You did? Wait, where did you see it?"

"Brianna has it," he said, wrinkling his nose.

So much for getting a sneak peek. Brianna, owner of Brides by Brianna and one of the newer wedding planners to join the scene, had hit our radar when she'd started spreading rumors about Wedding Belles in an effort to steal our business. Kate and Fern had retaliated by telling anyone who would listen that Brianna was, in fact, running a call girl business instead of planning weddings. From then on, we'd done our best to avoid each other.

I twisted around to see if I could glimpse our nemesis. Sure enough, she held court on a low tufted sofa setup near the DJ booth with a gaggle of twentysomething planners clustered around her, flipping through what was undoubtably the January issue of *Capital Weddings*. Before I looked away, Brianna caught my eye and glared at me.

"She does not look happy," I said, indicating her with a nod of my head.

Fern gave me an arch smile. "No surprise there. She's not on the list."

Kate sloshed some margarita on her sleeve. "She's not? I heard she campaigned hard this year. Cassie at the floral warehouse said she called them and begged them to vote for her."

"Sounds about right," I said, feeling more pleasure than I would have liked to admit that a planner like Brianna, who was short on substance and long on styled shoots, had been left off the list. "I'm surprised she didn't get her daddy to buy her way on."

Brianna's business had reportedly been bankrolled by her wealthy father, which meant she had money to splash out on advertising and expensive gifts for clients. There were whispers that's she'd recently passed out Louis Vuitton passport cases to all the hotel executives for the holidays.

"Money can't buy everything, darling," Richard said. "It certainly can't buy class."

"Congratulations," a young woman with glossy black curls said as she came up and gave Kate a hug. "Are you so excited?"

"Thanks, Sasha," Kate said, raising her cocktail in a salute. "It's always an honor to be on the list."

Sasha tilted her head at Kate then looked at me. "You don't know, do you?" She giggled and clapped her hands. "Wedding Belles got the star. You're top vote getter."

It took a moment for the news to sink in, but I felt my mouth drop open. Kate squealed as she bounced up and down, Fern taking the cocktail from her hand before it all spilled onto the marble floor.

Richard gave me a one-armed hug and cleared his throat. "Well, it could not be more well deserved."

"Thanks." I felt dazed. "I was afraid we wouldn't make the list because of all the drama at our weddings this year."

Fern waved a hand at me. "I mean, who doesn't have a few dead bodies pop up at their weddings?" He took a drink from Kate's glass. "The important thing is you always saved the weddings, even if it meant bending the law."

I hoped he would never mention that to my boyfriend.

"I wonder who else got stars," I said. Now I was dying to see the list and maybe stare at our star for a few hours.

"This is ridiculous," Fern said, handing both glasses to Kate. "I'll be right back."

He sashayed over to the planners huddled around the magazine. After talking to them for a few moments, they all jumped up and rushed across the hall. Fern picked up the abandoned magazine and hurried back to us.

"How did you do that?" Kate asked.

"Simple. I told them there was an Instagram wall they could take pictures of their cocktails against, and that no one had posted a cocktail shot yet." He winked. "It should take them a while to search the Cathedral and realize I lied."

I took the magazine from him and flipped to the back section where I knew the list would be. I located the section on wedding planners and ran a finger down until I found the blurb about Wedding Belles along with a hot-pink star. I felt a rush seeing it with my own eyes.

"I can't believe it," Kate whispered as she gazed over my shoulder at the magazine page. "Look at all the names of all those older planners around ours. I wonder what they think about this."

It hadn't occurred to me what the reaction from our competition might be, but as I looked up I noticed a group of older planners a few feet away giving us the serious side-eye.

Richard took the magazine from me. "Let's take a look at the list of caterers. Probably all the usual suspects."

I nudged Kate and indicated the glaring planners with a jerk of my head. "I'm not sure this is going to make us the most popular people."

"When you're on top, people are always going to want to knock you down." Fern took his cocktail back from Kate and raised it. "But at least you're on top, sweeties."

"We should go out and celebrate," Kate said. "And not in a place where they serve communion."

I felt my phone buzz and glanced at the screen. Why did Reese need me to call him ASAP?

"I think I'm going to faint," Richard said, the magazine slipping from his hand and dropping to the floor.

I caught his arm as he staggered against me. "What's wrong? Do you feel ill?"

"I'm dying." His words came out in short gasps as the color drained from his usually tanned face. "It's over."

Kate stared at her nearly empty glass. "What's happening? Was he poisoned?"

"Worse," Richard said, his eyes wide and his voice a strangled sob. "Richard Gerard Catering is not on the list."

CHAPTER 6

"*P*ut your head between your knees." Fern rubbed Richard's back. "It will help with the hyperventilating."

"We're in a car, you ninny," Richard said as he hitched in his breath. "I can't bend over that far without putting my head in the glove compartment."

I glanced at Fern in my rearview mirror and saw him make a face that Richard undoubtedly missed.

"Maybe that's where you should put it," Fern muttered.

Richard either didn't hear him or chose to ignore the comment. He slumped against the passenger side window of my car. "I can't believe this happened. My life is over."

I drove up the ramp of the National Cathedral underground parking garage and paused when we reached the top. Traffic on Wisconsin Avenue whizzed by us, allowing me to idle the car for a few moments. I cranked up the heat and put my icy fingers to the vents to warm them more quickly.

We'd rushed Richard out of the party and into my car so fast I hadn't had time to warm it up, so the air inside still felt like the air outside, and that seemed to be getting more frigid by the minute. "Your life isn't over. Like I said before, I'm sure you were left off the list by mistake."

"It's a conspiracy," Richard insisted. "I've been blacklisted; I just know it."

"Why would anyone blacklist you?" Kate leaned her head between the front seats. "Have you made any new enemies lately?"

"Of course not," Richard said, then tapped his chin. "Define 'enemies.' And 'lately.'"

As my car warmed, I took a long breath. "Why does it suddenly smell like I walked inside a gingerbread house?"

"Since we left the party in such a fast and furious flurry, I barely had time to eat." Fern held up a basket filled with cookies. "I might have grabbed a few treats for the road. Want one?"

"A few treats?" Richard gaped at him. "That's an entire basket of cookies from the dessert station."

"I wouldn't mind a cookie, " I said, reaching a hand behind me.

Richard looked at me like I'd just kicked his dog. "I can't believe you can eat at a time like this." His eyes flitted to the dark-brown cookie Fern put in my hand. "And those molasses cookies are meant to be paired with iced vanilla latte shooters."

My stomach rumbled. "I'll risk it."

A car honked behind me, and I looked up at the light, which was now green. I waved an apology and turned left into traffic, glancing over at Richard, who'd dropped his head into his hands. "I can't believe someone would have it out for you enough to remove you from the list. Everyone knows you're the best caterer in town."

I took a bite of cookie. Not only did it smell like Christmas; the sugar-dusted molasses cookie tasted like it. I could almost hear the sleigh bells as I wolfed it down. Kate and Fern both crunched on cookies behind me as well.

Fern held up the magazine in question. "He's definitely not on it. I've gone through the entire thing a few times." He flipped to a page and held it up. "I, however, got mentioned as an 'editor's pick'. What does that even mean? It's not like I've done any of the editors' hair." He flipped a few more pages to the masthead. "Or have I?"

Richard whipped his head around. "You brought that thing with you? I never want to lay eyes on it again for as long as I live. *Capital Weddings* is dead to me." He waved a finger in the air. "Dead, I say."

"At least you're not overreacting," Kate said.

Even though I agreed that Richard was being his usual overly dramatic self, I also knew that being left off the list was a huge deal and could mean that a lot of brides wouldn't be calling him over the course of the next twelve months. Unlike Wedding Belles, Richard Gerard Catering did more than weddings, but brides made up a big chunk of his client list. Not only that, weddings kept him from being bored to tears with corporate luncheons and drop-off deliveries to law firms. I, for one, did not want to deal with a restless Richard with too much time on his hands. I'd had a glimpse of it when he'd been shut down under suspicion of poisoning once, and I did not want to relive that anytime soon. I veered right onto Massachusetts Avenue as the light changed from yellow to red.

Richard clutched the armrest. "Where are we going? Georgetown isn't this way."

"We're stopping by the District Two police station," I said.

Richard snapped his fingers. "Excellent idea, Annabelle. I should press charges against *Capital Weddings*. This is slander and defamation at the very least."

I sighed. "We're not going to press charges against the magazine. Reese texted me and said he had some information about the baby that Buster and Mack found."

"Are we still going on about that baby?" Richard fluttered his hands in the air. "It's not like the child knows she's been abandoned. She's probably better off now than she was before. I, on the other hand, have had my entire reputation destroyed."

I hooked another right onto a mostly residential street and turned into the District Two parking lot. "I promise you we're not making light of what's happened, but I also promised Buster and Mack we'd help them find out as much as we could about who left Merry."

"It's not like we can't do both," Kate said. "We've investigated enough crimes that we should be able to juggle the baby case and figure out why you got left off the list."

Richard twisted to face her. "I do not say this often. "He paused. "Okay, I've never said this at all, but you are a genius, Kate."

She grinned. "Thank you. It's nice for you to finally ackno—"

He cut her off. "Don't let it go to your head, darling. It was probably a one-off, but you're right that we need to investigate why *Capital Weddings* has it out for me the same way we would a murder at a wedding." A flutter of the hand. "Or an abandoned baby."

"Fine." I let my breath out in a huff and stepped out of the car. Everyone followed me as I hurried across the parking lot out of the cold and into the two-story brown brick building with blacked windows. Reese was going to love this. Not only was I showing up with a small posse, I'd gotten roped into a second investigation. Maybe I wouldn't tell him about 'The Case of the Blacklisted Best Friend' right away.

I stamped my feet a few times to warm them up as we stood in the utilitarian foyer of the station. A reception desk to the right stood guard in front of a series of battered wooden desks behind it. I could hear the sounds of typing and of people talking. I spotted Reese bent over a desk looking at a computer monitor.

"It's been a while since I've been here," Fern said, slipping off his green-velvet gloves. "Do you remember the time I gave all the officers makeovers?"

"I don't think any of us will ever forget that," Kate said. "Especially the officer who got the Dorothy Hamill pixie cut."

Fern grinned and touched a hand to his own low ponytail. "That was very flattering for his face."

I led the way to the front desk and gave the female officer on duty my most winning smile. "I'm here to see Detective Mike Reese."

She stared at me, then her eyes shifted to my friends. Her stony expression didn't change. "He expecting you?"

"He's probably not expecting all of this," Kate said under her breath.

"Tell him his friend Richard Gerard is here," Richard said.

We all looked at Richard.

He shrugged. "What? We did a lot of male bonding yesterday. You can really get to know someone when you pick out a Christmas tree with them."

After their exhaustive tree search, I was pretty sure Reese felt that he knew more about Richard now than he ever wanted to.

Reese looked up and saw us. I waved at him and assumed a look of oblivious innocence. As I saw him raise an eyebrow, I felt sure it hadn't worked.

"So," he said, walking over to us, "the gang's all here."

"We were at a party at the Cathedral when you texted me," I said. "It was quicker to bring them with me."

Reese pushed up his already rolled-up shirt sleeves. "Come on back. I want to show you something."

The female officer at reception grudgingly lifted the swing gate so we could follow Reese.

"So I pulled all the security camera footage from any business near the Born Again Biker Church." He rested a hand on my back as we gathered around a desk with him. "It's in a strip mall that hasn't gone through gentrification yet, so not all of the businesses have cameras, and those that do have them don't keep them on all the time. That being said, I did manage to get one feed that shows us the front of the church."

He typed something on his keyboard and a video began playing full screen. It was black and white and pretty grainy. It also appeared to only film every few seconds, so the footage looked jerky. We all leaned in to watch the view of the front of the church from a side angle. The glass double doors opened and closed a few times as churchgoers appeared to leave. I glanced at the time stamp. Around twelve thirty on Sunday afternoon. This would have been after the service ended, so we were probably watching the last stragglers. Several minutes passed on the video time stamp, and then a figure moved into the screen holding something. I heard myself suck in breath, and I saw Kate raise a hand to her mouth.

The figure, who wore a dark coat and a scarf covering their face, placed a baby carrier outside the door. Even with the delayed time and jerky footage, I could see the hesitation as the figure gazed down at the child before knocking on the glass and turning away quickly. Then the figure was gone from the screen, and the next thing we saw was the large figure of Mack coming outside and finding the baby.

Reese reached down and stopped the video. Fern sniffled and produced a handkerchief from his pocket, then dabbed at his eyes. I found myself blinking away tears as well.

Richard cleared his throat. "At least they had the good sense to knock on the glass. Considering how cold it was yesterday, the little thing could have frozen to death if no one knew to look for her."

"It was someone who cared about her." I leaned closer to Reese and felt comforted by the warmth of his hand on my back.

"Whoever it was, they had second thoughts," Kate said, her voice breaking.

I nodded. "You could see them hesitate."

"Too bad we can't tell anything about them from the footage," Reese said. "The face is completely covered, and they turn away from the camera when they leave."

"We know it was a woman," Fern said.

We all turned to him.

"We do?" Reese asked.

Fern pointed to the screen. "Back it up a bit." When Reese rewound the footage, Fern waved his fingers. "See? Right there. A bit of her hair flies out of the scarf when she turns."

Reese bent his face near the monitor. "Well, would you look at that?"

"Just because they have long hair doesn't mean it's a woman," Richard said. "Have you seen the hair on some of Buster and Mack's biker friends?"

Fern let out a short breath and pointed to the strand of blond hair on the screen. "It's also color treated. How many Harley riders get highlights done?" He held up his hands. "Not that I'm saying they couldn't use some face-framing color."

"Are you sure?" I asked.

Fern folded his arms over his green velvet jacket. "As sure as I am that you haven't had a haircut in six months, and Kate is about a week away from needing her roots touched up."

"I'd take his word as expert testimony," I told Reese.

CHAPTER 7

J ran the last few steps down the sidewalk and pushed through the glass doors of Lush, the bell above me ringing as I stamped my feet on the concrete floor to regain feeling in them. Kate and Richard were close on my heels, and I could hear Kate's teeth chattering as she unwound the scarf from her neck.

We'd dropped Fern at his salon on the way after he'd remembered he had a full afternoon of society matrons who needed cut and color. We'd promised to fill him in on any new information on the search for the baby's mama, and he'd promised Richard he'd keep his ear to the ground about any catering gossip.

"I haven't been here in ages," Richard said, walking further into the flower shop. "It's like stepping into a greenhouse."

I had to agree with him. Between the almost tropical heat, which must have been turned to full blast, and the heady perfume of flowers spilling out of the galvanized metal buckets lining the wall, it felt like we'd entered a hothouse. The back metal table held a bubble bowl with a partially finished holiday arrangement of red roses and holly leaves with remnants of trimmed flowers scattered around it. I noticed a pair of empty cappuccino cups on the table alongside a baby bottle.

Mack appeared from the doorway that led to the back of the shop. He was decked out in his usual black leather pants and leather vest with chains that jangled as he walked. The only addition to the outfit was a black baby carrier attached to his chest, and I could see Merry's chubby legs dangling beneath. Part of me was surprised the baby carrier wasn't leather with his biker club's emblem emblazoned on the front.

He held a finger to his lips. "She just fell asleep."

I tiptoed toward him and peered at the tiny face pressed sideways against his T-shirt. "How long will she sleep?"

Mack shrugged. "Two hours? Two minutes?" He rubbed his eyes, and I could see how bloodshot they were. "We haven't exactly worked out a sleeping schedule yet."

Richard sniffed. "It doesn't smell like a baby in here. You must be doing something right."

Buster emerged from the back holding a plastic container of Lysol wipes and rubber gloves. "We aren't getting much floral designing done, that much I can tell you."

"Are you positive you want to take this on?" Kate reached out and touched the baby's tiny pajama-clad foot. "There are some wonderful foster parents out there."

Mack's face darkened. "No foster care."

"We didn't come to talk about Merry," I said. "Well, not directly at least."

"If you're calling about the changes for Saturday," Buster said, holding up a yellow-gloved palm, "I already know. Darla called me an hour ago."

"Darla called you?" I pulled my phone out of my purse. "She didn't call me. What changes? It's only a few days before the wedding. There can't be any more changes."

Kate waved a finger at me. "That right there is why Darla

didn't call you. I'll bet she knew you'd tell her no, but she thought she could sweet-talk the boys."

I couldn't imagine what additional changes they could have come up with only a day after we'd had the final meeting. I dropped my phone back in my purse. "Well? Did she sweet-talk you?"

Buster set the Lysol wipes on the metal worktable. "Unfortunately for her, sleep deprivation does not make me more open to last-minute changes." He took off his rubber gloves. "Who needs a coffee besides me?"

Kate and I both raised our hands.

"It makes him a bear," Mack said in a stage whisper with an apologetic smile to Buster. "Well, it does."

Buster grunted at him as he moved in front of the large cappuccino machine and began fiddling with nozzles. "Debbie saw some Instagram post about holiday margaritas and wanted to add some mistletoe for garnishing."

"I wonder what the bah humbug bride thinks about that," Kate said.

I turned to Richard who was staring down at his phone. "It must have been the mistletoe margaritas from the Cathedral party. I can't believe she saw posts from it so soon."

"Believe it," Richard muttered. "All anyone is posting is either closeups of their cocktails from the party or pictures of their listing in *Capital Weddings*."

Mack's face lit up. "Is the new list out already?"

"That's right." Buster turned from measuring coffee grounds. "I'd forgotten it should be hitting the stands soon."

Kate shook her head while I made a frowny face. Both floral designers looked confused.

Richard sighed. "Oh, for heaven's sake. My career may be finished, but I haven't gone blind." He glanced back at his phone screen. "That's it. I need to call my office."

49

He walked a few feet away and leaned against a high top table, his phone pressed to his ear.

"Richard Gerard Catering wasn't on the list," I said in a low voice, even though the sounds of Buster's fancy machine made it pointless for me to whisper.

"What?" Mack looked from me to Kate. "That's impossible. He's one of the top caterers in town. He's been on the list since they started it."

"It's true," Kate said. "Not only did he not get top vote getter like he did last year, but his name doesn't appear on the list at all."

Buster glanced over our heads at Richard. "I'm surprised he's so calm."

"He was less than calm when he found out," I said. "Actually, he shrieked and wailed so loudly we had to remove him from the OWP holiday party before security dragged him off."

"That sounds more like Richard," Mack said, jiggling the baby as she shifted in the carrier.

"So," I said, realizing we'd drifted way off topic, "what happened with Darla?"

Buster handed Kate and me each an oversized white cup topped with frothy white foam. "Before I could give her my answer, she got squirrelly and hung up the phone."

"I wonder if the bride busted her," Kate said as she blew on her cappuccino.

I wrapped my hands around the round coffee cup so my fingers absorbed the warmth. "All I know is that if the bride spots a mistletoe margarita, it's going to be a very one-sided wedding."

"What kind of lunatic plans a December wedding when they hate winter and winter holidays?" Kate asked.

"We don't know if she hates all winter holidays." Buster twitched one broad shoulder up and down. "Maybe she'd be up for using blue and white and decorating with dreidels. Hanukkah is very overlooked when it comes to design inspiration."

"From my short experience with this bride, I'm guessing that wouldn't fly either," I said, "although an ice-blue winter wedding would be stunning."

"That's it," Richard rejoined us. "My career in this town is over. I'm kaput, done, finito."

Mack thumped him on the back and he staggered forward. "It's only one issue of one magazine."

Richard waved his phone in the air. "I just called into Richard Gerard Catering HQ and there has not been a single new inquiry since this morning."

I glanced at the modern chrome clock on the wall and took a tentative sip of coffee, so I wouldn't burn my tongue. "It's only one o'clock."

"But it's the holidays," Richard said. "These are our busiest weeks. We make more money in December than in any other month."

"Odd how your business picks up and ours slows down," Kate said.

"That's one good thing we can say about weddings," I said. "Not many in the dead of winter."

The Douglas wedding was an anomaly. Rarely did we take weddings around the holidays because it was the one time of year we weren't insanely busy. Of course, Darla and Debbie were repeat clients, and they never capped their budgets, two reasons we'd agreed to a wedding right before Christmas. Part of me wished we hadn't, though, because I didn't like having to finalize wedding details when I should be focused on decorating my tree and picking out presents. I hadn't even gotten a present for Reese, and I knew if I didn't act fast I'd be either paying for overnight shipping or giving him coupons for free hugs.

"But you have a lot of corporate parties coming up, right?" I asked as Richard paced small circles in front of me and muttered to himself.

Richard stopped pacing. "For now. What happens when the magazine actually hits the stands and word gets out I've been kicked off the list? This is a fickle town, Annabelle. One day you're hot and the next you're . . ."

"Listen." I set down my cup and put a hand on his arm. "None of your regular clients will stop using you because of some silly wedding list."

Kate added her hand to mine. "Don't forget that we promised to help you find out who's behind you getting taken off the list. If there's a conspiracy, we'll get to the bottom of it."

"That reminds me." I took my hand off Richard's arm and reached into my purse for the image Reese had printed off for me. I held it up to Buster and Mack. "Does this woman look familiar?"

Mack squinted at the grainy black-and-white photo. "That's a woman?"

"Fern confirmed it from the blond hair popping out of the scarf," Kate said.

Neither man questioned Fern's assessment as they leaned in to study the image.

"This is the person who left baby Merry in front of your church," I told them. "Reese pulled footage from a nearby security camera, and it shows this woman putting the baby down and walking away."

"This must be her mother," Buster said, touching his pointer finger to the image. "And she has blond hair."

Mack looked down at the tiny head lolling against his chest. "That makes sense. Merry has fair coloring, although her hair is just peach fuzz right now."

"Do you know anyone who could be this woman?" I asked.

Buster shook his head. "It's hard to say. Aside from the blond hair, there isn't much to go on. You can't see anything of her face except the tip of a nose and even that's blurry."

I looked at the grainy image. He was right. Although we now

knew the person who abandoned Merry was a woman with blond hair, that only narrowed the field down to tens of thousands of people in the DC area.

"It was a long shot," I said, setting the photo down on the nearby worktable. "What we really need to do is what the cops do —inspect the scene of the crime."

"You mean the place where the little waif was left?" Richard asked. "What do you think you'll find? A driver's license the woman dropped and nobody noticed?"

I ignored Richard's snarky comments. "From the video, we can tell what direction she approached from. It would be helpful to see where that is and what's there."

"You want a tour of the Born Again Biker Church?" Mack asked.

"That can be arranged." Buster pulled out a key ring. "Since we're deacons, I have a key."

"What are we waiting for?" Kate rubbed her hands together. "I've never been to a biker church."

Mack motioned to Merry with his head. "I'll stay here with her and mind the shop. There's no way I'm taking her out of this carrier now that she's actually sleeping."

Buster led us toward the front door, but Richard didn't follow.

"You coming?" I asked, looking back at him.

"I'll stay with Mack," Richard said, throwing an arm around the florist's wide back and not reaching the other shoulder. "I have a few things to check out online anyway."

I couldn't help being suspicious. Since when did Richard voluntarily hang out with a baby and a florist?

"Suit yourself," Kate said, tugging me by the sleeve.

As I walked through the glass door Buster held open, I cast a final glance at Richard and Mack, an odd couple if ever there was one, and hoped my gut feeling was wrong.

CHAPTER 8

"This definitely doesn't look like any church I've ever seen." Kate peered up at the sign stretching across the storefront of the worn-down mini mall. "Born Again Biker Church" was written in dark block letters with a red cross on each end of the sign. This was a far cry from the picturesque wooden clapboard churches or impressive stone cathedrals we usually found ourselves working in.

I'd parked my CRV in one of the spaces that butted up to the glass-fronted church, glad not to have to parallel park on the street for once, and I joined Kate on the sidewalk. I twisted to look at the businesses around us. The area was still mostly low warehouses and strip malls with operations not looking for much walk-by traffic: commercial kitchens, car repair shops, off-site storage. I knew that rent in this area of the city was lower, so spaces were larger and a little run-down.

I pulled the photo of the woman out of my purse and arranged myself at the proper angle. "She came and went from this direction."

Kate held a hand over her eyes as she followed my gaze across the parking lot. A three-level self-storage complex and street parking were the only things in that direction. "Unless the woman lives in a storage unit, I don't think she came from there."

I put the photo back in my purse. So much for that bright idea.

Buster roared into the lot and angled his bike in one of the motorcycle spots at the end of the row. He took off his black skullcap helmet as he got off his bike and walked toward the double doors with keys in hand. We huddled behind him to block the wind as he jiggled the keys in the glass doors.

He finally pushed one side and held it open for us. "We don't keep the church unlocked if there's no service. Not that we have anything worth stealing."

"That's an understatement," Kate whispered to me as we hurried in out of the cold.

The inside of the church was as utilitarian as the outside with a dingy tile floor, metal folding chairs arranged in uneven rows, and a few sagging sofas around the edges of the room. Near the doors were a pair of spindly-legged rectangular tables stacked with pamphlets and Bibles, and a round table held a pair of coffee dispensers with paper "Caf" and "Decaf" signs taped on the front. Styrofoam cups held sugar packets and wooden stirrers, and a clear plastic bin of cookies looked to be mostly crumbs. The scent of coffee, evergreen, and sweat lingered in the air, which was quite a change from the aroma of incense and flowers I associated with churches.

Buster flipped a switch by the door and long rows of fluorescent lights on the ceiling flickered to life. "It's not much, but the folks who come here don't worry too much about appearances."

Despite the bare-bones decor and odd combination of smells, there was a warmth to the place I couldn't explain. A Christmas tree strung with popcorn chains stood in one corner, and shiny-gold garland hung in swags over the low stage at the front. I walked over to a large bulletin board hanging on the wall. Newspaper articles about the church's philanthropic activities were tacked up alongside fliers selling bikes and notes with messages of encouragement from one member to another. I turned and looked out the glass front of the building and noticed the transparent surface was hazy.

Buster saw me studying it. "We put an anti-shatter film over the glass."

"Why?" I asked, touching my fingertips to the cold surface.

Buster shrugged. "Some groups don't like the work we do. They don't consider us real Christians because it's our policy to love and accept everyone and not to judge."

"Who would have a problem with that?" Kate asked. "Love and acceptance sound pretty churchy to me."

He pointed to the newspaper clippings on the bulletin board. "We've gotten some press for the funerals."

Kate and I went over to the board. I scanned one of the articles. "So you set up human shields outside of funerals?"

Buster rocked back on the heels of his leather boots. "You know those churches that like to hold up hateful signs when it's a funeral for a suicide or a gay person or even a soldier? We make sure the family and friends don't have to see any of that ugliness."

"I had no idea you and Mack did that." I felt embarrassed I'd known them for almost five years and had never been aware of this part of their lives.

Buster shrugged. "Like I said, we don't believe in judging. We know what it's like to be judged. Most of our members have done plenty of things they aren't proud of, and most of the world would judge them harshly for. But we've all seen our way to the light. Now we're about spreading that light."

Kate pointed to an article on the wall. "You guys escorted this kid to school when he was being bullied?"

Buster grinned. "That was one of my favorites. His grandmother is one of our members and told us how bad he was being picked on. About thirty of us rode him to school and dropped him off so all the other kids could see. We even got him his own leather vest. I don't know if I've ever seen a kid smile so much."

I could imagine that an escort of over two dozen rough-looking biker dudes on Harleys would make most bullies think twice.

Kate reached for a napkin from the coffee station and dabbed it to her eyes then nudged me. "Why don't we do something like that?"

"That was a good day." A man with a grizzled gray beard and leather jacket came inside, stomping his feet on the doormat. A skinny woman with dishwater-blond hair was with him and as she took off her scarf, I noticed a colorful tattoo swirling up from the cleavage exposed by her leather lace-up vest.

Buster gave the man a handshake and one-armed hug. "Hey, Soul Man. I was showing my friends around. They're helping us find who left the baby." He kissed the woman on the cheek. "Hey, Shelley."

The older man nodded, his eyes going to us. "Welcome to our church." He stepped forward and held out his hand. "I'm the preacher. Everyone calls me Soul Man. And this is the missus."

The woman winked at us. "Call me Shelley." Her voice made her sound like a two-pack-a-day smoker, but she smelled like tea rose perfume when she leaned close.

"Annabelle," I said, shaking both of their hands. I motioned to my assistant who was blowing her nose. "This is Kate."

Kate waved as she wiped her nose with the limp napkin. "Buster was telling us about the work you do."

Shelley walked over to the coffee station and began straightening the supplies. She handed Kate another napkin. "How are y'all getting along with this baby thing?"

"We don't know much," I said. "Except that a woman dropped her off."

Shelley moved her head up and down. "Makes sense. It was probably the mama who got scared and didn't know what to do."

"You don't know any of the wives or girlfriends of church members who might have been pregnant, do you?" I asked.

"Not many come to services," Soul Man answered for her. "We might only have a handful of women each Sunday; ain't that right Shelley?"

"Sometimes it's just me and Christie Gail," Shelley said. "That's our daughter."

Buster and Soul Man moved across the room and started moving the folding chairs back into straight lines.

"Do you ever get together with the other wives and girl-friends?" I asked.

"When we do group rides, more of them turn out," she said. "And everyone shows up for the picnics. Me and Soul Man don't go out as much anymore, but some of the men play pool down at Bedlam."

"Bedlam?" Kate asked.

"A bar in Adams Morgan where a lot of bikers tend to hang out." She looked us up and down. "But you could go if you wanted to. They have a vegan menu."

I didn't ask why one look at us made her think we would be vegans, and I tried not to act surprised that a bar frequented by bikers would have an animal-product-free menu in the first place. These Harley riders were more complicated than I'd given them credit for.

Shelley jerked her thumb toward a pair of doors on the other side of the room. "I'm gonna hit the ladies."

When she disappeared into one of the doors, I turned to face Kate. "Are you thinking what I'm thinking?"

"That we have *got* to see what they put on a vegan menu at a biker bar?"

I waved one hand at her. "No, although I'd like to meet some of these vegan bikers. I'm thinking maybe we should find out more about their daughter."

"You think she could be the one who dropped off the baby?" Kate dropped her voice. "Wouldn't her parents have noticed?"

"You've heard of the teenaged girls who wear baggy sweat-shirts and no one even knows they're pregnant," I said. "It's been sweater weather for almost four months now."

"You're only saying this because she's the only other female we've heard about who's associated with the church," Kate said.

"Probably," I admitted. "But it's worth at least checking out. If she looks anything like her mother, she'd have blond hair."

Shelley emerged from the bathroom, and I waved her over. "You don't happen to have a picture of your daughter, do you?"

She reached into the back pocket of her jeans. "Sure I do, hon." She pulled out a small rectangular picture and held it out. "This isn't all that recent, but you can see she takes after me."

Kate craned over my shoulder to see. "She's adorable. How old is the photo?"

I stared down at the school photo of a little blond girl who could not have been over ten-years-old.

"It's from the beginning of the school year," Shelley said. "She's cut her hair since then."

I handed it back to her. "She's your only daughter?"

Shelley sighed as she tucked it back in her wallet. "Soul Man and me got a late start, so she's all we got. She's enough though."

"She's not boring you with baby pictures, is she?" Soul Man asked, wrapping an arm around Shelley's waist as he and Buster rejoined us.

Shelley slapped his chest. "They asked to see a picture of Christie Gail."

Her husband raised an eyebrow.

"It's true," Kate said. "We love kids."

I made a point not to look at Kate and see if her pants were on fire.

"Well, I'd better get back to Mack." Buster jangled the keys in his hand.

I remembered that Richard stayed with Mack and the baby, and wondered what the three of them had been up to while we'd been away. I was almost afraid to find out.

We said our farewells to Soul Man and Shelley outside the church while Buster locked up. As Kate and I walked to my car, I felt my purse vibrating. I dug my phone out and looked at the screen. Richard.

"We're on our way back," I said when I answered.

"I'm not at Lush anymore," Richard said.

I hesitated at my car door. "Where are you?"

"I'm going right to the source, Annabelle." Richard's voice was a couple of octaves higher than usual.

"The source of what?" I asked, ignoring the sound of Kate yanking on her door handle on the other side of the car.

"I'm outside the offices of *Capital Weddings*," he said. "I'm about to march inside and demand to know who has it in for me."

I groaned. This was not going to turn out well.

CHAPTER 9

I spotted Richard on the corner of I Street looking up at a glass-fronted office building with his arms crossed. Even though the wind whipped down the street and swirled my long hair into my face, Richard's short spiky hair was unruffled.

"What are you doing out here?" I asked as Kate and I hurried up to him. "You're going to freeze to death."

"I can't feel a thing," Richard said, his eyes not leaving the building. "I'm fueled by outrage."

"That's not a good sign," Kate said.

I followed his gaze. "So what's the plan? Are you trying to hex the staff at *Capital Weddings* from out here?"

He gave me a sidelong glance. "Don't be absurd."

This from the man who'd been known to have voodoo dolls made to look like people who'd offended him.

The glass door to a nearby Starbucks opened, and the scent of coffee wafted over to us, along with a blast of heat, both welcome as we stood outside in the cold. A woman in a puffy black jacket passed holding a red cardboard cup covered in snowflakes, and I looked at the tall cup longingly. I wouldn't mind ducking inside and getting a peppermint mocha, but I couldn't leave Richard.

"What happened to hanging out with Mack?" I asked. "Or was that all a ruse so you could come down here before I could talk you out of it?"

"If I hadn't wanted you to know I was here, I never would have called you," he said. "But you know there's only so much baby I can handle at a time. Once the little creature woke up, it was time for me to go."

"Why don't we discuss your plans for revenge over coffee and scones?" Kate asked, taking a step toward the Starbucks.

"I've abandoned my quest for revenge," Richard said.

"That was fast," Kate said, giving me a look that told me she didn't believe him. Knowing Richard, I wasn't convinced either.

"Right now I just want to know what happened." Richard's brows pressed together to form a wrinkle between his eyes. "I couldn't have gone from top caterer to off the list in the course of a year without reason."

"I maintain it could have been an error," I said. "You know the magazine's been using more and more interns to do their fact-checking."

"Then I'd like to meet the intern who was so bad at their job they forgot to list the city's best caterer." Richard squared his shoulders and headed for the entrance of the building.

Kate and I rushed to follow him, more for the intern's sake than anything else. We passed through the glass doors of the office building and crossed mouse-gray marble floors to a bank of elevators. Richard threw his arm out to catch a set of closing doors, and we hopped on behind him. There were only two men inside with us, and they both wore dark suits and power ties. We all faced forward.

"Don't you want to know what we discovered at the Born

Again Biker Church?" Kate asked Richard in a low voice as the elevator surged upward.

"Do I have a choice?"

Kate ignored his comment. "To be honest, it was a bit of a bust. There's nothing but self storage in the direction the woman came from, and Soul Man and Shelley couldn't think of any women they knew who'd been pregnant."

One of the men in the elevator glanced over at us, but Kate didn't seem to notice.

"Soul Man?" Richard asked.

"The preacher," I explained. "Shelley is his wife. They were both very nice."

"So you're back to square one?"

"I don't think we ever got very far off square one," Kate said. "Annabelle thinks we need to meet more of the church members."

The elevator doors opened and one of the men stepped off, glancing back at us as he left.

"It's clearly connected to the church or someone who goes there," I said. "You have to go out of your way to find the place, so only someone with a strong connection would seek out a biker strip mall church in Northeast DC."

The other man raised his eyebrows as he stared down at his newspaper.

"We're going to go check out Bedlam," Kate said. "It's a biker bar in Adams Morgan where some of Buster and Mack's church friends hang out."

Richard twisted to face me. "You're going to a biker bar?"

"You should come with us," Kate said. "They even have a vegan menu."

"Vegan food at a biker bar?" Richard shuddered. "Perish the thought."

The elevator dinged and the doors opened.

"This is us," Richard said, striding off without a backward glance.

We followed him to the right where he threw open a set of glass doors with the words "Capital Weddings" written across them in swirling black letters. A sleek half-moon reception desk sat in the small lobby with two groupings of white furniture and copies of *Capital Weddings* magazines scattered across a glass coffee table.

A blond receptionist looked up at us and smiled. "Can I help you?"

"I certainly hope so," Richard began. "I've come to lodge a com—"

I stepped in front of him. "We'd like to speak to your editor in charge of the 'Best of' list. We don't have an appointment."

Her smile had faltered when Richard had started in on what was clearly meant to be a tirade, but she regained her sunny expression. "Of course. Let me see if Marcie is available. Who should I tell her is here?"

Richard opened his mouth, but I cut him off. "Annabelle Archer from Wedding Belles."

She seemed to recognize the name and nodded as she picked up her phone. I motioned for Richard and Kate to follow me to one of the sofas.

"Why didn't you let me talk?" Richard asked.

"Because you would have made that poor girl cry, and she had nothing to do with the list," I said, keeping my voice to a whisper. "Besides, if there really is a conspiracy against you, we don't want them to know you're here. This way we still have the element of surprise."

Richard sniffed and brushed the arm of his jacket. "I guess living with a detective is rubbing off on you, darling. You're getting positively sneaky."

I'd take that as a compliment and as an indication that Richard was getting used to the idea of me living with Reese.

"Annabelle!" A tall woman with jet-black hair appeared from around the corner. "I can't believe it's actually you. This is such good timing."

I stood up and accepted her hug, even though I didn't think I'd ever laid eyes on the woman. "Is it?"

She bobbed her head up and down. "I was going to ship you a box of magazines since you were one of our top vendors. Congratulations, by the way."

"Thanks." I swept a hand behind me. "Have you met my assistant, Kate, and my friend, Richard?"

Richard extended his hand in front of Kate. "Gerard. Richard Gerard." He gave her a pointed look. "As in Richard Gerard Catering."

"So nice to meet you both." Marcie shook his hand and then Kate's, but didn't seem to register anything when Richard said his company name. "Why don't you come back to my office, and we'll get you those magazines."

Richard held me back as we followed Marcie out of the lobby and into an open floor plan office with a hive of cubbies. His face looked distressed. "She didn't even recognize my name."

"It's not like she actually works in our industry," I said to him in my softest voice. "They may have a magazine about weddings, but when have you actually seen any of these people out at our weddings or industry events?"

Richard scanned the room even though we saw mostly the tops of heads and a few clusters of people talking. "Then why are they making decisions that affect all of our careers?"

"That's the million dollar question," I said.

Marcie paused when she reached an office in the corner with glass walls and floor-to-ceiling windows overlooking I Street. She waved at a pair of chairs across from a wooden desk. "Have a seat."

Kate and I sat while Richard hovered behind me. Marcie walked behind her desk and pressed an intercom button on her phone. "Marcus, can you bring me a box of our January issue?"

"Marcus?" Richard asked.

"He's my right-hand man." Marcie sat in her leather chair. "He's been with me for a few months now, and I couldn't have put the last issue together without him."

"Was he involved with gathering information for the list?" Richard asked.

Marcie tilted her head at Richard. "Actually he was. He took over most of that, which was amazing since it's such tedious work. How did you know? Do you know Marcus?"

"Here are those issues you requested." A young man with wavy blond hair entered the office, holding a cardboard box.

"I do know Marcus," Richard said, his hands on his hips and his eyes blazing.

Marcus saw Richard and dropped the box. It landed on his foot with a heavy thud, and Marcus shrieked in pain.

CHAPTER 10

"So Marcus worked for you?" I asked after Kate had found us a small table at the back of the Starbucks on I Street. We'd hustled Richard out of the *Capital Weddings* offices after his screams had started to gather a crowd. Marcus rolling around on the floor clutching his possibly broken foot hadn't helped matters.

Marcie had stood gaping while Richard hurled accusations of slander and defamation at the injured man until Kate and I had finally managed to drag him off. I'd have to call her later and apologize for the chaos and thank her for the magazines. I pushed the cardboard box under the table.

Richard slumped into his chair. "For almost a year. I brought him on to try to ease some of my workload."

"He's cute," Kate said, then shrugged when Richard glared at her. "What? He is. I mean, from what I could see before he started screaming and rolling around."

"Why don't you get us some coffees?" I said to her and held out my Starbucks card.

She waved me off and tapped her phone. "I use the app. This one's on me."

As the warmth from the coffee shop defrosted my fingers and toes, I slipped off my coat and hung it on the back of my chair. "So clearly it didn't work out. What went wrong?"

"It started when Babette began ordering too much food," Richard said.

I looked at him. "Babette?"

"From the movie *Babette's Feast*. That's what I called him when he ordered enough food to feed the entire city for a dinner party for ten."

"You don't have a nickname for me or Kate, do you?" I asked.

"You mean like Laurel and Hardy, Punch and Judy, Laverne and Shirley?"

I leaned back. "Yes, like that."

Richard straightened. "Of course not, darling."

I wasn't sure if I believed him, but I also wasn't sure if I wanted to know. "So he ordered too much food, and you fired him?"

"No. That was only the beginning, even though I had to talk our chef out of murdering him when our food costs went through the roof," Richard said. "He didn't take direction well and saw himself as a creative visionary instead of my assistant."

I could see how that would cause problems since Richard considered himself a creative visionary, and his company certainly wasn't big enough for two.

"So you guys didn't get along well. That's not unheard of in the wedding world. Why did it end so badly?"

"Do you remember my big corporate client?" Richard put his elbows on the small round table and rested his chin on his hands. "The one who gave me a few events every month?"

"I remember you mentioning them," I said. "Drop-off lunches, board meetings, annual holiday parties."

Kate returned carrying a cardboard holder with three large holiday cups covered with white plastic lids. "Peppermint mocha for Annabelle, a caramel brûlée latte for Richard, and a sugar-free nonfat no whip vanilla latte for me." She slapped a brown paper bag on the table. "And some scones. This occasion calls for carb loading."

Richard took the cup she proffered. "Do you think you could have come up with a more pretentious coffee order?"

"Absolutely." Kate winked at him. "I could have asked for soy milk."

"So, the corporate client?" I prodded, taking a sip of my minty mocha and enjoying the full-fat, sugar-filled, whipped-cream-topped coffee.

"Right," Richard said as Kate sat down. "I guess Marcus felt he wasn't getting the respect or creative license he deserved, so he changed one of my proposals that went out to my bigwig client."

"Changed it how?" Kate opened the paper bag and took out a scone.

"Added so much profanity it would have made a sailor blush."

I almost choked on my drink. "To a catering proposal?"

"Yep." Color filled Richard's cheeks. "Every other word was an F-bomb, and the descriptions of the food were so dirty I couldn't even understand half of them."

"That is dirty," Kate said with wide eyes as she put a piece of scone in her mouth and crumbs fell onto her lap.

"So you fired him?" I asked.

"Spectacularly," Richard said. "I told him he'd never work in the event industry again, but I guess I didn't consider that he'd go work for a magazine about the event industry."

Kate took a long sip and dabbed at her upper lip, even though she had no whipped cream to dab off. "Are we sure he left your name off the list on purpose?"

"You saw the way he reacted to seeing Richard." I tore a corner off of Kate's scone. "He looked as guilty as anyone I've ever seen."

"Marcus is smart, even if he can't cater to save his life." Richard drummed his fingers on the table. "It's clear to me he maneuvered his way into the magazine, made himself indispensable, and then took over the list. He played the long game without anyone knowing it."

I chewed on my bite of cinnamon scone and thought for a moment. Richard's version of how it had played out seemed pretty convincing to me, and it was the only reasonable explanation as to why Richard Gerard Catering would be omitted from a list they'd topped for years.

"So what can we do about it?" Kate asked.

"The better question is how can we make it look like an accident?" Richard asked.

I shushed him as Kate giggled. "You know we shouldn't even be joking about that."

"Just because people tend to drop dead around us?" Kate asked. "If you think about it, it's the perfect cover. The police are used to us finding murder victims. They never expect us to produce one."

I shot her a look. "I still don't think we should joke about murder. Especially not one in which Richard would be the primary suspect."

Richard frowned. "That does put a damper on my plans."

"I'll call Marcie and talk to her after things have cooled off a bit," I said. "I'm sure once I explain you were left off the list and why her assistant might have been motivated to leave you off on purpose, she'll understand."

"But what can she do?" Richard threw his hands in the air. "It's not like they can reprint thousands of copies." He paused. "You don't think they'd reprint it, do you?"

I shook my head. "Nope."

His shoulders slumped. "So that's it then. Even though I was knocked off the list by a vengeful former employee, there's nothing I can do about it. Even if the magazine issues an apology or prints an addition in a future issue, I'm still not on the list for an entire year."

I patted his hand. "I'm really sorry, Richard."

"You know what would make you feel better?" Kate said, her eyes bright.

"I'm almost afraid to ask," Richard said.

"You should come with us to Bedlam." Kate rubbed her hands together. "It'll take your mind off all of this."

"I'm sure the last thing Richard wants to do is hang around a loud bar with a bunch of bikers," I said.

Richard sat up. "I don't know. Maybe a biker bar would be fun."

I tried to keep my mouth from dangling open.

Richard tapped his chin. "The more I think about it, the better it sounds. How long have I been working myself to the bone to build up my business? Years." He snapped his fingers. "And it can all be taken away from me like that."

"It hasn't all been taken away from you," I said.

"First, I lost my biggest corporate client, and now I stand to lose a significant amount of wedding business." Richard smacked his hand on the table. "If anyone deserves a night to cut loose, it's me."

"That's the spirit." Kate smacked her hand on the table as well.

Richard stood up. "If we're going to Bedlam tonight, then I need to dash."

I glanced at the clock on the wall. "We still have a few hours."

"Not if I'm going to put together an appropriate outfit," he said. "I'm not sure what kind of shape my leather is in."

"Leather?" My voice came out a squeak.

Richard waved his fingers up and down in front of me. "If

we're going to do this, we're going to do it right. Don't even think of wearing a sweater set and pedal pushers, darling."

I opened my mouth to say that I didn't own a pair of pedal pushers, but Richard was already flouncing out of the coffee shop.

"This should be fun," Kate said.

This should be a disaster, I thought.

CHAPTER 11

"*J*'m not so sure about this." I tugged at the shimmery-black miniskirt and felt glad I'd paired it with black tights. At least they kept my legs somewhat warm, which was more than I could say for the red sequined tank top. I rubbed my arms as I hurried along behind my assistant.

"You look great." Kate turned and flicked her eyes up and down my outfit as she walked ahead of me on Eighteenth Street. "My clothes almost look as good on you as they do on me."

I dodged a few people as I tried to navigate the sidewalk behind her in heels. "I still insist what I had on was fine."

Kate shot me a look over her shoulder. "Sure it was, if we were welcoming a classroom of first graders back to school." She swept an arm wide and almost belted someone. "This is Adams Morgan. Home of hole-in-the-wall restaurants and grimy bars."

I glanced around at the jumble of neon signs illuminating the dark and the lines snaking out of basement entrances. The air smelled of ethnic food and pulsed with the sounds of club music. I turned as we passed a townhouse with two lines—one leading upstairs to a brightly lit bar called "Heaven" and another twisting down to a dark club glowing with red light and a sign indicating "Hell." Eighties music spilled out of Hell along with college-aged kids.

"I'm definitely having second thoughts," I said, stepping over a puddle of something unidentifiable on the sidewalk.

Kate stopped as we reached a nondescript building with the word "Bedlam" hanging above the door in Gothic letters. "I thought you wanted to help Buster and Mack find the baby's mother."

"You know I do," I said. "I'm just wondering if there's a way that doesn't involve me showing so much skin."

"We usually do things your way." Kate patted my arm. "Tonight we're trying the Kate method of investigation."

Usually Kate's method of anything involved lots of flirting and not much else.

"As long as we actually do some investigating," I said as I eyed the dark bar with the heavy wooden door.

Kate winked at me. "Follow my lead."

I trailed inside after her and paused for a moment to let my eyes adjust. Even though it was nighttime, the street outside was bright with street lamps and neon signs and headlamps from passing cars. Inside Bedlam, the lights were dim and the furnishings were dark. Tall black leather banquettes lined the walls, which were made of dark wood paneling. A lamp hung over a pool table in the back, and a long mahogany bar stretched down one side of the place dotted with leather-topped barstools. I didn't notice any Harley-Davidson signs, but most of the patrons lounging at tables and clustered around the pool table looked like versions of Buster and Mack.

Kate sashayed up to the bar and hopped onto a barstool, ordering a beer for each of us before I'd figured out how to sit down without my skirt riding up to my belly button. I decided to lean against the bar instead.

The bartender, who had a gray mustache that curled up at the ends, set two bottles in front of us and his eyes settled on me. "You girls sure you aren't looking for Heaven and Hell?"

I laughed, trying to sound causal. It came out sounding strangled. "We're friends with Buster and Mack. And Soul Man."

The bartender raised a bushy eyebrow and nodded. "None of them are here tonight, but some of the other boys are." He gestured toward the group playing pool.

"Thanks." I took a swig of beer and tried not to grimace as I swallowed it. Beer was not my drink of choice and especially not domestic light beer. I pulled one of my heels off the sticky floor. I suspected more beer had been spilled on the floor at Bedlam than had been drunk.

Kate leaned in to me. "Good thing Richard isn't here. He'd run out of hand sanitizer within five minutes."

I feared she was right. "He said he'd meet us here, but maybe he changed his mind."

"I'll bet dollars and doughnuts he's home plotting revenge," Kate said.

"Dollars *to* doughnuts," I corrected, but without much enthusiasm. Richard had been as disheartened as I'd ever seen him this afternoon, and I hoped he wasn't home alone getting more depressed.

"Well, smack my tush and call me Judy!"

Kate and I both turned toward the familiar voice. I squinted at the men playing pool and shook my head. "Is that . . .?"

"It sure is," Kate said, gaping at the lean man dressed head to toe in black leather. "How did Richard beat us here?"

"I don't know, but it looks like he's been here for a while."

Kate watched Richard high five the burly men he was playing with. "And I think he's winning."

I pulled her with me as I walked over to him. As we got closer, I could tell that his leather was shiny and unmarred, unlike the other men whose jackets and vests were worn and dull and covered in patches. There was a distinct possibility that Richard had gone out and purchased his outfit right after we'd left him. Not that I had any clue where you bought biker wear in Washington.

"Annabelle! Kate!" He beamed at us and raised a beer bottle. "You made it."

I was speechless. Not only was Richard dressed in leather and playing pool with a bunch of bikers, he was drinking beer out of a bottle without wiping the top first. Things were worse than I'd thought.

"Are you okay?" I asked.

He waved a hand at me. "I'm better than okay. I'm great." He jerked his head toward the three men standing with him. "Slim, Stray Dog, and Rubble have helped me realize that I was upset over nothing."

I glanced at the men and nodded greetings. "Thanks for helping him out, guys."

"Don't mention it," the biggest man said, thumping Richard on the back. "We know what it's like to be in a low place."

Had Richard told them details or had he been vague? I doubted men named Stray Dog and Rubble had ever fallen into a funk over a listing in a wedding magazine.

Richard grinned at the man. "Slim here is one of the deacons at Buster and Mack's church. He's very wise."

I noticed that Richard was slurring his speech and wondered how many beers he'd put away before we arrived.

"You two are friends with Buster and Mack?" A man with heavy stubble and a black T-shirt stretched tight over his belly switched his pool cue from one hand to the other.

"We're friends from work," I said. "Do you all go to the Born Again Biker Church?"

The men nodded. Jackpot.

"Crazy about the baby, isn't it?" Kate asked as she leaned one hand against the edge of the pool table.

The men murmured agreement.

"Any idea who could have left her?" I asked.

They shook their heads.

"We don't got many female members," Slim said. "And if any of our members got some girl in trouble, I hope he would have come to us. We don't judge each other. We get enough of that from the outside world."

The shortest and stockiest man leaned down on the pool table to take a shot. "Most of us got girlfriends or wives now."

"Rubble's right," the stubbly man said. "I can't think of a one of us who's still out there playing around."

"Any thoughts about who might have had reason to leave their baby at your church?" I asked.

Slim tilted his head for a moment before raising and lowering one beefy shoulder. "Can't think of anyone." He looked at the man with the five o'clock shadow. "Stray Dog? You're tight with the younger guys."

Stray Dog frowned. "You got me. I don't think I've laid eyes on a pregnant lady in months."

"So much for that," Kate said to me.

A cocktail waitress in black shorts and a spaghetti strap white top slapped a laminated menu on a nearby high top table. "Y'all want any food?"

Kate picked up the menu while the blond waitress tapped her toe impatiently. "I might give the grilled vegan wrap a try."

"Grilled vegans?" Richard made a face. "No thank you."

I looked over Kate's shoulder. "It's made with portobellos, not actual vegans."

"That sounds only slightly better," Richard said.

"We should probably be going," I said, noticing Richard leaning against Slim.

LAURA DURHAM

Richard blew a raspberry. "Nonsense. The night is young. Live a little, Annabelle."

"I, for one, want to see what Richard's like when he cuts loose." Kate handed the menu to the waitress. "We'll get the Mexican pizza to share."

Richard shook his hips. "Ole'!"

Oh boy.

"You sure we're not gate crashing?" I asked Slim.

"Naw," he said. "It's not like you're the only outsiders here." He pointed over my shoulder. "I think those two are lost."

Richard's glazed eyes popped open. "I must be losing my mind."

I swiveled my head and stifled a groan. Kate inhaled sharply beside me. "Is it too late to hide?"

"There you are, dearie!" Leatrice called out as she thrust a hand high in the air to wave as the other hand held Fern's arm.

"I'll race you out the back," I said.

CHAPTER 12

"What are you wearing?" I asked Leatrice when she and Fern joined us.

She spun around and the bright-red felt skirt belled out around her. The skirt was decorated with vividly colored sequined appliqués of nutcrackers, angels, and wrapped presents. "It's called a Christmas tree skirt. Do you like it?"

"You're wearing a Christmas tree skirt?"

Leatrice looked at me like I was a simpleton. "Well, it is the Christmas season. This is a very popular item on the Home Shopping Network. I'm sure you'll see other people wearing them around."

"I doubt it." I didn't have the heart to break it to her that the skirt was meant to wrap around the base of a Christmas tree. At least she was in season.

"Fern said we were going to a restaurant, so I thought I should dress up." Leatrice glanced around her, then lifted her red cowboy boots off the sticky floor one at a time. "Restaurants downtown sure have gotten casual."

"How did you know we were here?" I asked Fern.

He wore a pair of black jeans and a white T-shirt with what appeared to be a pack of cigarettes rolled up in the sleeve. His hair, usually tied back in a bun or ponytail, was brushed up into a pompadour with a ducktail of dark hair flipped up at the nape of his neck. "Kate texted me."

I narrowed my eyes at her.

"What?" She dropped her voice. "I didn't know Leatrice would tag along. Or dress more like a drag queen than him."

I pointed at the cigarettes in Fern's sleeve. "Since when do you smoke?"

"I don't." He grinned and flexed an arm muscle. "This is my 'bad boy' look since my leather was at the cleaners."

Did everyone own leather except for me?

"What are you drinking, little lady?" Slim asked Leatrice.

She blushed. "Well, aren't you the gentleman? I'll have a Shirley Temple with extra cherries."

Fern winked at him. "Make that two, sweetie, but instead of extra cherries I'll have extra vodka."

Slim ambled off to the bar while Rubble and Stray Dog resumed their game of pool. As I cast a glance at my ridiculously dressed friends, I mentally declared the evening a bust. We'd only met a few members of the Born Again Biker Church, and we didn't have leads on any new blondes who may have left baby Merry on the doorstep. I had to admit to myself that the baby may have been left at random, and there was a distinct possibility we'd never track down the mother. I felt a twinge of sadness for the baby, but reminded myself that she was currently being spoiled to death by Buster and Mack.

"We're heading out pretty soon," I said. "Richard's probably reached his limit."

Fern did a double take as his eyes rested on Richard slumped against a pool cue. "I didn't recognize him without his school-marm posture."

"He's self-medicating," Kate said in a whisper that was anything but. "After the fiasco with C-A-P—"

"I may be bereft and without a reason to live," Richard interrupted her, straightening up, "but I have not lost my ability to spell, thank you very much." He tried to put one hand on the pool table in a jaunty stance but missed and stumbled against Kate.

As the pair almost tumbled to the floor, I shook my head and jerked a finger toward the bar. "Let me stop Slim from ordering those drinks. I don't want to have to carry anyone else out of here."

I sidled up to Slim as he leaned against the mahogany bar with one booted foot resting on the brass railing at the bottom. He nodded at me.

"Is it too late to cancel those orders?" I asked. "I probably should get my friends home."

"Nix those drinks, Francie," Slim called out to a thin woman at the other end. The burly bartender who'd been working when we'd entered must have gone on break. The thirtysomething woman now tending bar wore a bright-white T-shirt over tight jeans, and her lips shone with coral-pink lip gloss.

The woman walked down to our end and ran a hand through the frosted hair that fell in feathers around her face. "Even the club soda with lime?"

Slim gave a gruff laugh. "Naw. Keep that."

The woman winked at him, filled a rocks glass with club soda, dropped a lime in it, and passed it across the bar. "Don't drink it too fast, big guy."

Another laugh from Slim as he took a swallow.

"I'd better settle my tab," I told the woman, pulling out some folded bills I'd tucked in my pocket earlier.

Slim waved my money away. "I got it. Any friends of Buster's and Mack's are friends of mine."

"That's very sweet," I protested, "but you don't need to do that."

He nodded at the bartender. "It's done." He cut his eyes to Richard behind us. "And both of the drinks the nervous fella had."

"Richard only had two drinks?" I asked.

"The first one was a boilermaker, so that may have been the problem," Slim said. "Your friend isn't much of a drinker, is he?"

"Not unless it's champagne or fine wine," I said, wishing I'd been there to see Richard drop a shot of whiskey into a beer mug and drink them both. I could count on one hand the number of times I'd seen either beverage pass his lips. And I'd have fingers to spare.

Slim studied me for a second. "Buster and Mack haven't brought you on a ride along, have they?"

"A ride along?" I asked, shaking my head. "On their bikes?"

"We got a bunch more church members who aren't here but who'll be at our event tomorrow." Slim tossed back the rest of his club soda and spit the chewed up lime into the bottom of the glass. "Meet us at the church parking lot at ten a.m. and you can hop on the back with a couple of us and see what we do."

"What do you mean?" I asked, my heart already racing at the thought of riding on the back of a Harley. It made me nervous just to look at them, much less ride on them.

"We're providing protection for a funeral tomorrow." Slim thunked the glass on the bar. "You want to know what we're really about, that's where you'll learn."

"Okay," I said before I could think better of it. I did want to meet more church members, and after reading about what the church did to help people they thought were unfairly judged, a part of me wanted to see these reformed bikers in action. "We'll be there."

Slim grinned at me and then looked at the bartender. "We'll make her a biker chick yet, Francie."

The bartender looked me up and down as Slim walked back to the pool table. "You won't find better men than Slim and his boys."

"We're friends with Buster and Mack," I said, hoping their names gave me some instant street cred I was lacking.

Recognition flashed across her face, and she nodded. "They don't come in here much, but they're good people."

I watched her flick a pale strand of hair off her face. "Sounds like you've known the Road Riders for Jesus for a while."

"We get all kinds in here, but they're special." She popped the cap off a Bud Light bottle and slid it over to me. "On the house."

The last thing I wanted was another beer, but I raised it and thanked her as she moved off to the far end of the bar. I took as small a sip as humanly possible and stared at the woman's frosted blonde hair, wondering if there was any chance she'd been the one to leave the baby on the doorstep of the church she clearly admired.

CHAPTER 13

"*W*hy is there so much light?" Richard groaned as he dragged a blanket over his head and rolled over on the couch.

I padded into my living room, dodging the hanging paper stars, and set a mug of coffee on the coffee table for him. "Maybe because it's morning?"

"Impossible," Richard mumbled from under the beige cashmere throw. "I just fell asleep. At least I think I did. The details are a little fuzzy."

I popped the top on one of the bottled Frappuccinos I depended on to give me my morning caffeine and sugar rush and sat across from him in the yellow twill chair, tucking my bare feet under me to keep them warm. "I'm sure they are. You refused to leave Bedlam without doing a shot of tequila with Stray Dog."

Richard threw the blanket back and sat up. "That's absurd. When have you ever known me to do a shot of . . ." He raised a hand to his forehead. "Oh, good heavens. Did I suffer a head injury last night?"

I took a swig of my cold mocha drink and let my eyes close for a moment as I swallowed. I may not have liked to drink regular coffee, but add chocolate, lots of sugar, and milk, and I was hooked. "Like I said, there was tequila."

He blinked a few times, moving his hand over his eyes to block the light streaming in from the tall windows on one side of the room. "Who's Stray Dog?"

"According to you, he's your new best friend," I said, grinning.

Richard flushed and his eyes caught the pile of black leather clothes folded over the far arm of the couch. "It's starting to come back to me."

I motioned to the coffee mug. "Reese thought you might still be in need of sobering up."

Richard began to reach for the coffee and froze. "Reese?"

My boyfriend walked into the room, his own travel mug in hand. He wore gray pants and a black half-zip sweater, and his hair still looked damp from the shower. "Look who's alive."

Richard pulled the throw up higher over his bare chest and managed a weak smile. "Good morning, Detective. Fancy meeting you here."

Reese took a drink from his tall cup, and the corner of his mouth twitched up. "Just what I was thinking."

Richard gave him a manufactured laugh, his cheeks reddening even more.

"You have to go in to work?" I asked Reese.

"In a bit." His eyes flitted to Richard. "I thought I'd head out and give you two some time alone."

"Very considerate of you," Richard said.

I drained the last of my bottled coffee and stood. "No need. Kate and I are heading out on a ride with the Road Riders for Jesus."

Richard blinked at me rapidly, taking in my jeans and snug-fitting white T-shirt with the Wedding Belles logo on the front. "You and Kate are riding Harleys now? How long was I out?"

"Are you sure about this?" Reese asked, taking hold of one of my belt loops and pulling me close. "Not that it isn't sexy to think of you on the back of a motorcycle, but are you sure this is safe?"

The thought of riding on the back of a Harley still made my stomach flutter, but I pushed aside my nerves and nodded with more confidence than I felt. "It's the best way to meet more people who're connected to the church. Anyway, I'm not going alone. Kate will be with me."

Reese raised an eyebrow. "That doesn't make me feel any better."

"Kate's better than you'd think in pressure situations," I said. "You can't work on weddings for so many years and not be."

A phone trilled and we all looked around. Reese touched his back pocket and shook his head. "Not mine."

Richard hunted around in the folds of the blanket until he found his ringing phone, cleared his throat, and answered it. "Richard Gerard Catering. This is Richard."

I turned to Reese as Richard began talking in his most official voice to someone who was clearly a client. "I thought of something last night. Is there any way to do a search of local hospitals and see who's given birth in the past month?"

"I'm assuming this means you've turned up nothing?" he asked. When I didn't answer, Reese angled his head at me. "You're kidding about the hospitals, right?"

"Why not? If we had a list, we could find out if each mother was in possession of her baby."

"First of all, there are quite a few hospitals in the metro DC area. More if you include the suburbs." Reese counted off a finger and then raised another one. "And secondly, there are privacy laws. I can't go pulling birth records all over the city for something that isn't even an official case. I'd like to keep my job if you don't mind."

Well, when he put it like that.

86

Richard hung up and dropped his phone on the couch. "Are you still going on about that baby?" He stood and wrapped the throw around himself, throwing one end over his shoulder. "I'm telling you, Annabelle, as much as I'd love to see the little poop machine exit our lives as quickly as possible, you're looking for a needle in a haystack."

"Richard's right," Reese said. "The chances of locating the woman who left the child are slim. She abandoned the baby for a reason, and she clearly doesn't want anyone to know. I hate to think of the child being orphaned, but if her parents don't want her, she may be better off finding a family that does."

Richard made a surprised little noise. "Would you look at that? The two men in your life agree on something."

I wasn't sure what it said about me that one of the most important men in my life stood wearing a cashmere throw as a toga, but I didn't dwell on it. If I was being honest with myself, I knew they were both right. So far we had almost no leads, and it felt like we were shooting in the dark.

"I promised Buster and Mack that I'd try," I said. "I owe it to them."

Reese crossed to the coat rack in the corner and plucked his leather jacket from one of the hooks. He held it out as I slipped my arms inside. "If you're going to do this, you should do it right."

Even though it was a little big on me, the well-worn leather held traces of my boyfriend's aftershave. I popped the collar. "Better?"

"Heaven preserve us," Richard muttered, scooping up his own leather clothes from the end of the couch.

Reese pulled me to him by the collar, and my body pressed against his. "I'm digging this bad girl look. You sure you have to leave right now?"

"At least wait until I do," Richard said as he clucked disapprovingly.

Reese kissed me a bit more intensely than usual, then released me. I tried to catch my breath as I felt the heat creep up my face. I cleared my throat and turned to Richard, trying to act like I wasn't flustered. "Are you sure you're okay about the whole *Capital Weddings* thing? You're not going to rush off and try to blow up their office while I'm gone, are you?"

"Old news, darling," he said with a wave of his hand. "I've got more things to do than plot revenge on my old employee Marcus."

I suspected revenge was still on the to-do list even if it had moved down a few notches. "Like?"

"For one, that was Darla on the phone, and she wants all the dishes with cranberries, nutmeg, and nuts to be removed from the menu. Actually, it's the bride who wants to commit this travesty. Now I have to figure out how to rework the menu so it isn't bland and boring."

Even though he was complaining, I knew he liked being tasked with a challenge. I liked the fact that it would take his mind off 'the list.' "If you've already prepped some of the food with festive flavors, we could always use it for our team holiday party on Thursday."

"Thursday?" Richard nearly dropped his armful of clothes. "We're throwing together a party in two days?"

"It's just our crew," I said. "Nothing fancy."

Richard gave me a disapproving look. "Just because it's small, doesn't mean it shouldn't be done properly." He tapped his chin. "It's too late for custom signage, but I could probably come up with a signature cocktail. And we need a theme. Maybe Christmas in Caracas or a Hannukah in Havana?"

"The theme is 'old wedding stuff," I said. "I've got an office filled with leftover cocktail napkins, stir sticks, striped paper straws, and favors that I never want to see again. We're going to use it all, so if you can come up with a drink that works with that, be my guest."

Richard looked aghast for a moment, then he cocked his head. "It's so horribly kitsch, it could work."

There was a knock on the door and Reese opened it. Kate stood in the doorway in hip-hugger jeans and a Wedding Belles T-shirt that matched mine peeking out from under a brown leather bomber jacket. Her usually smooth bob was tousled, and dark eyeliner made her eyes look smoky. "Ready to ride?"

Richard gave her the once-over. "The descent from Wedding Belle to Hell's Angel didn't take long."

Kate winked at him. "You should join us on the dark side."

"Not on your life," Richard said with a sniff. "I have to redesign the wedding menu for your Scrooge of a bride, plus the detective and I have plenty to do here to get this place ready for the holiday party."

Reese's head swiveled to him. "Wait? What?"

"I certainly can't do it all by myself," Richard called over his shoulder as he headed down the hall with his clothes, dragging the blanket behind him. "You do live here now. That makes you one of us."

"Look at the bright side," I said as I stepped into the hall with Kate. "You seem to be 'in' with Richard."

Reese let out a deep sigh as he watched me go. "Talk about a double-edged sword."

CHAPTER 14

"*I*'m starting to feel guilty," I said as Kate swung her car into the parking lot of the Born Again Biker Church. "Do you think I should have left Reese with Richard? You know how he gets when he's on a tear about something."

"Oh, I know how Richard gets." Kate turned off the car engine and opened her door. "If I were you, I'd be more concerned that Reese might shoot him."

"That's very comforting," I said, getting out and following Kate toward the people clustered around the shiny-chrome Harleys in front of the church. Each bike had a large American flag attached to its bumper that waved in the wind.

I felt a nervous flutter as I took in the number of tattoos, piercings, black bandanas, and leather in the group. Most of the men had either sun-weathered faces or beards, and the women showed cleavage or midriffs or both, despite the cold weather.

I spotted Slim, and he waved a hand in greeting as we approached. "You made it. Wasn't sure if the idea of a bunch of bikers might have scared you away."

"We're tougher than we look," Kate rested one hand on her jutted-out hip.

"We work with brides," I said. "Not much scares us anymore."

Slim chuckled. "Fair enough. You're with me and she's with Stray Dog." He handed us both black skullcap helmets before hooking one over his own head. He threw a leg over the seat of a low motorcycle and motioned behind him. "Hop on."

I watched Kate jump on behind the stubbly younger man from the bar as he revved his engine. I eyed Slim's bike for a second before taking a deep breath and straddling the seat behind him, the large flag at my back. He gunned the motor, and I threw my arms around his waist seconds before we lurched forward. As the other bikes around me roared to life and we left the parking lot in a double line, I pressed my eyes closed.

Since we were still in the city, I knew we weren't going very fast, but the heavy vibration of the bike and the throaty rumbling of the engine made me tighten my grip. I felt the wind whip my face and cut through my jeans as we accelerated. I opened my eyes long enough to see we were heading out of DC, then I closed them again. As I concentrated on breathing and trying not to freeze to death, I huddled behind Slim and felt grateful that he wasn't so slim.

After a while, the bike slowed, the wind died down, and Slim leaned into a turn. I blinked a few times as we pulled up to the entrance to a cemetery and tried to loosen my grip on the big man in front of me. I heard Kate whoop as the entire procession of bikes rolled to a stop.

"That was amazing," she said, running up to me and thumping me on the back. "Wasn't it?"

I pulled off my helmet and tried to force my frigid lips into a believable grin. "Amazing."

Slim twisted around and winked at me. "You don't look too worse for wear."

I peeled myself from the leather seat and held onto the back of the bike for a moment, feeling like my entire body was still vibrating. "I'm good. Thanks."

"Cheese and crackers! Annabelle? Kate?"

Mack's voice made me turn. "Surprise," I managed to say in a steady voice.

The burly florist gaped at us, his mouth a perfect circle surrounded by his dark-red goatee. "What are you two doing here?"

"What do you think?" I asked. "We're trying to gather more information about anyone who might have left baby Merry, remember?"

Mack's eyebrows lifted, then his eyes slid away from mine. "Of course. I guess I didn't know you were so determined."

Kate elbowed him. "You know Annabelle once she gets her teeth into an investigation."

"So no luck so far?" Mack asked.

"Not really," I admitted. "My only lead is Francie at Bedlam."

"The bartender?" Mack asked. "I don't know if you talked to her for long, but she's not the maternal type."

"All the more reason she'd want to give up a baby," I said.

Mack looked at me like I'd lost my mind. "If she'd gotten pregnant, maybe, but that skinny thing hasn't gained a pound in all the time I've known her."

I felt deflated, even though I knew she'd been a long shot.

Kate put an arm around my shoulders. "I guess it's back to the drawing room."

"Or the drawing board," I said and couldn't help noticing Mack trying to hide his pleasure.

Before I could ask him if I was wasting my time searching for this mystery mother, I heard loud voices from across the street.

Mack's face darkened. "Diddly darn, those people make me so mad I could spit!"

Knowing Mack and his aversion to cursing, these were harsh words. I followed his narrowed eyes to the small group of protestors across from us holding neon-hued signs and chanting behind a police barrier.

Kate put a hand over her mouth. "Those signs are horrible. What's wrong with those people?"

Mack's eyebrows pressed together. "That so-called church thinks they have the right to pass judgment on the entire world."

I glanced behind me at the gravesite with a dark-green tent erected over several rows of chairs. Sprays of white flowers on stands crowded the gravestone. "Whose funeral is this?"

"A soldier killed in combat," Soul Man said, joining us. His wife stood a few feet away talking to some of the other women.

I felt a lump in my throat and rising fury at the protestors. "So what do we do?"

The biker preacher crossed his arms over his chest and jerked his head toward the small but noisy group. "Since we've been invited by the family, we're going to move a row of bikes in front of them so the family can't see or hear the protest when they arrive."

I balled my hands into fists and felt my planner instinct kick in. "Let's do it."

Slim nodded at me and got back on his bike with me behind him. Stray Dog and Kate followed us and about ten other bikers as we positioned ourselves in front of the meager protest. The shouts were louder since they were right behind me, and I twisted to see a wiry gray-haired man shaking a sign so close I could have reached out and grabbed it. I fought the instinct to snatch it from him and whack him over the head.

"I'll stay on the bike and rev the engine as needed," Slim said. "You take the flag and stand in front of me to block the view."

As I jumped off the bike and pulled the flag from its holder, I glanced up and saw the woman next to the gray-haired man staring at me. Unlike the frenzied man beside her, she didn't shake her sign and she wasn't screaming. She looked like she wanted to be anywhere but there. But she was there, I reminded myself, and I wondered if she felt any shame at what she was doing. I gave her what I hoped was a look of disgust and returned to my task, lifting the flag and walking to stand in front of Slim.

Mack backed his bike next to Slim's and took his own flag from the back, standing next to me as the striped fabric snapped in the wind around us.

"I'm assuming Buster is watching Merry," I said, making my voice a near shout to be heard over the motorcycle motors and the protesters.

He nodded. "This is no place for a baby."

I agreed. I wondered how much longer they would be content juggling a newborn, a thriving business, and their Christian biker gang.

"Did you just poke me?" Kate's shriek rose above the noise.

I turned to see a protestor with a bad perm and dark roots that made her look like a blond skunk holding a sign inches from Kate. Before I could remind Kate that the Road Riders for Jesus were a nonviolent Christian biker gang, the woman jabbed Kate so hard she stumbled back and fell into Stray Dog's lap.

So much for a nice ride in the country, I thought as chaos erupted around me.

CHAPTER 15

"*W*hat on earth happened to you two?" Richard asked as Kate and I walked in the door to my apartment, his head peeking over the open divide between my living room and kitchen.

I sniffed the air and almost coughed as I inhaled the heavy scent of cinnamon. "Are you baking?"

He walked out holding a wooden spoon. "No, I'm mulling spices." He waved the spoon in the direction of Kate's face and the faintly purple mark on her left cheekbone. "Should I get a steak for that bruise?" He glanced at my filthy T-shirt. "And some Spray-and-Wash for that shirt?"

"Do I have steaks?" I asked, wondering if he'd taken it upon himself to stock my kitchen like he used to do back when I was single.

He gave a small snort as he shook his head. "Of course not. Your kitchen is a wasteland. It took all my creativity to pull together the mulling spices."

"I'm fine," Kate said, heading for the couch and shrugging off her bomber jacket. "You should see the other chick."

Richard raised a perfectly arched eyebrow. "I take it the ride didn't go well?"

"The ride was great," Kate said. "We just had a bit of a disagreement with the people protesting the funeral."

Richard looked bewildered, so I brought him up to speed on the funeral and the protesters and the melee that the police broke up and Slim and Stray Dog had to drag Kate out of.

"It sounds like you were on the side of right," Richard said, appraising Kate with a look of admiration. "Well done, darling." He turned his eyes to me. "And where were you while Kate was channeling her inner lady wrestler?"

"Annabelle tried to help, but she got tangled up in the bikes," Kate said.

That was a gracious way of saying I'd tripped and fallen flat on my face in the dirt. Mack had finally picked me up, rescuing me from being trampled to death by everyone running to the fight. By the time I'd gotten my bearings and recovered from being stepped on by more than one heavyset biker, the brawl had been over.

Richard patted my arm then wiped his hand on the Santa Claus apron tied around his neck. "Better luck next time."

As far as I was concerned, there wouldn't be a next time. As good as it made me feel to act as a human shield for the soldier's funeral, I'd come to one definite conclusion. Harleys were not for me. I could understand why people loved them, and I didn't deny the rush I'd gotten from the roar of the motor coursing through my body, but the bad-ass bikes made me feel a little *too* invincible. Another few rides on a cruiser, and I was afraid I'd be putting my difficult brides in headlocks.

I breathed in again as I slipped off Reese's leather jacket. "Do I smell curry?"

Richard spun on his heels and returned to the kitchen. "Like I said, I had to improvise. It did give me a brilliant theme for our holiday party though."

I wiped the last traces of dirt from my boyfriend's jacket as I hung it back on the coat rack and exchanged a glance with Kate. Every holiday season Richard decked out his offices in his own totally unique spin on a theme that over the years had ranged from Bolshevik glamour to Tibetan chic.

"Didn't we agree the theme was leftover stuff from past brides?" I asked.

"That doesn't have much of a ring to it," Richard called after he pressed the automatic ice maker, and I heard the freezer spit out a few cubes. "But Taj Ma-Holidays does, doesn't it?"

Taj Ma-Holidays? Kate mouthed to me.

Richard's head appeared over the dividing counter. "As in Taj Mahal. Get it?"

Oh, I got it.

"We can serve Curry Kwanza cheese puffs, Merry Mango lassies, and Dreidel Dreidel Dahl." Richard clapped his hand. "I've planned out a menu that covers every winter holiday."

Kate sighed. "What's wrong with crantinis and cutout cookies?"

Richard sucked in air. "I guess nothing if you want to be predictable."

"Do you remember what happened to your creative holiday decor last year?" I asked, flopping down in the chair across from Kate.

"You mean my Christmas in the Casbah, an Arabic interpretation of the holidays?" Richard marched out and handed Kate an ice pack wrapped in a red-striped dish towel. "It would have been worthy of *Architectural Digest* if Jim's insane flying squirrel hadn't destroyed it."

"Your catering captain brought Rocky to the office again?"

Kate sat forward as she touched the ice to her bruise. "I don't think I heard this."

"Really?" I muttered. "He complained about it for weeks. At least it felt like weeks."

Richard shot me a look. "That flying rodent scattered the sand I'd put around the Christmas tree so it would look like it was sitting in the desert. The sand dunes were ruined. Then he ran up the tree and clung to the very top, bending it over until it almost touched the floor before he jumped off. Of course the tree snapped back, and my camel tree topper flew across the room and crashed into the bay window. Not to mention the tiny Bedouin ornaments that fell all over the floor." Richard stifled a small sob. "It was awful."

"Which is why we should keep things simple," I said. "The party is in two days, and we have the Douglas wedding on Saturday. I, for one, would *not* like to add anything else to my plate. Let's do a grab bag gift exchange, drink some bubbly, and reminisce about our craziest brides of the year."

Kate raised a hand. "I second that. We also have this baby situation we promised Buster and Mack we'd help them with. There's no time to build a Taj Mahal out of sugar cubes or whatever you might be envisioning."

Richard opened his mouth to protest, then tilted his head. "I never thought of a sugar cube Taj Mahal. I wonder—"

"No!" Kate and I said in unison.

Richard jumped. "Fine. We'll do your repurposing theme and serve gingerbread and champagne with cranberries for garnish." He pretended to be snoring then jerked awake. "Oh, I'm sorry. Did I fall asleep out of boredom?" He turned and stomped back to the kitchen.

"I think we can cross 'tracking down the missing baby mama' off our list," I said, making a point of ignoring Richard slamming around in the kitchen.

"You're giving up so soon?" Kate asked. "It's only been a few days."

I looked down at my dirt-smeared shirt. "And we've gotten nowhere. No potential moms. No witnesses. No nothing. I'm starting to think whoever left baby Merry did it randomly and just got lucky Buster and Mack found her."

Kate didn't look convinced. "Maybe, but I still think a biker church in a run-down strip mall is an odd place to dump a baby."

"I also get the feeling that Mack doesn't want us to find the mom," I said. "He seemed practically pleased when I told him we'd had no luck so far."

"They do seem pretty attached to the baby," Kate said. "The longer she stays with them, the worse it'll get."

I held up both palms. "I'm not going to be the one who tries to take her from them."

Kate switched her ice pack from one hand to the other. "If we don't find the mother, they're going to have to notify social services. You can't just keep a baby like that."

Especially since my boyfriend was a cop and knew the entire situation. Even knowing how broken the system was, Reese wouldn't be able to look the other way for much longer. I guess I understood, even though it was hard to imagine two people taking to the role of instant parent better than Buster and Mack. I hated the thought of how broken-hearted they'd be.

"I guess we're going to have to wish for a Christmas miracle," I said.

Kate winked at me. "Here's Taj-Ma-hoping."

"I heard that," Richard yelled.

CHAPTER 16

"So explain this grab bag gift exchange thing to me again," Kate said the next morning as we strolled through Georgetown.

Wreaths made of fake greenery with a shiny-gold bow tied at the bottom topped each of the streetlights dotting the sidewalk down M Street, and the steady ringing of a bell told me a Salvation Army bucket was nearby. The sidewalks were crowded with shoppers, so I held my to-go peppermint mocha close to keep it from getting knocked out of my hand.

I stepped around a sandwich board sign advertising 30 percent off, hearing the holiday Muzak spilling out of the designer handbag store, and giving Kate a tug as she slowed to look at the pricey purses. "We each buy a present under twenty dollars and wrap it up, then at the party we sit in a circle, and the first person picks a present and opens it."

"Sounds simple enough so far."

I pulled the collar of my coat tighter around my neck, regretting not wearing a scarf to block the wind. "The next person can either 'steal' that present or open a new one."

Kate fell behind me to avoid a harried-looking mother pushing a double-wide stroller. "What happens to the person whose gift was stolen?"

"They open a new one."

Kate fell back in beside me. "Why do I have a feeling this is going to end in someone getting their knickers in a fist?"

"You mean knickers in a twist?" I asked as Kate mouthed the phrase to herself then shrugged. She made a good point. This had the potential for drama.

"Every time I've done it at a party, it's been fun," I said, taking a sip of my now-lukewarm peppermint mocha.

"Were Richard and Fern at any of those parties?"

I slowed as we passed Starbucks and breathed in the rich scent of coffee. "Well, no, but even without the gift exchange, there's a good chance one of them will flounce off in a huff about something."

Kate raised a finger. "Point taken. So we have to find something under twenty dollars that anyone at the party might like?"

"That's the idea." I looked down the brown paving stone sidewalk at the red-brick and cream-colored townhouses pressed up against each other in a row, their colorful awnings hanging over glass fronts. Some of the buildings rose two stories and some three, giving the rooftops an uneven, jagged look. I wondered if any of the stores contained a gift that would appeal to both Richard *and* Buster or Fern *and* Mack.

I ducked into The Paper Source and pulled Kate with me. "Let's look in here."

We pushed through the tall doors and past the rows of chic wrapping paper hanging on wooden rods. Tables were piled high with books, crafting kits, and oversized mugs, and it smelled of paper and ink.

Kate picked up an adult coloring book featuring sea creatures on the cover. "Does Reese like dolphins?"

"Very funny," I said, taking a final drink of my coffee and tasting the bitter dregs from the bottom of the cup. I'd almost forgotten my boyfriend would be at the party and that he'd mentioned it to his older brother, Daniel, a former cop we'd gotten to know during a few past weddings that had taken a turn for the deadly. I decided not to mention that to Kate since she'd been known to flirt shamelessly with Daniel and had even once planted a serious kiss on him. Knowing he might be at the party would distract her from the task at hand.

I held up a box of hands-free walkie talkies. "This might work for Leatrice."

Kate sighed. "That's right. Leatrice is coming."

"Do you really think we could sneak a party past her eagle eyes?"

Kate grasped my coat sleeve. "Do you think she's bringing Sidney Allen?"

I hadn't thought about that, but now that Kate mentioned it, I felt sure Leatrice would bring the prima donna entertainment designer she'd been dating. "There's a decent chance of it."

Kate held up a box with a colorful drawing of three llamas on the front. "How about Llamanoes? It's like dominoes, but with pictures of llamas in funny outfits." She picked up a small set of fabric dolls with yarn hair. "And these are like voodoo dolls. Richard would love them. I'm sure he's worn out the ones he has."

I was sure he had. "Let's not encourage Richard to stab imaginary people any more than he already does."

Kate replaced the dolls on the table. "Good point. So far Llamanoes are the gift to beat."

I raised an eyebrow. This was not going to be easy. I wandered around the store and was inspecting a set of stemless champagne flutes when Kate glided up to me.

"Pssst," she said without turning her head to look at me. "I think we're being followed."

I swiveled my head to her. "Followed? What are you talking about?"

"Don't look at me," she scolded. "Act natural."

I fought the urge to roll my eyes. "And standing next to each other and talking without looking at each other is natural?"

She motioned toward the large glass front of the store. "Don't be obvious, but I'm pretty sure that man was walking behind us earlier."

"So?" I peered across the open space at the short figure in a heavy brown coat and black knit cap standing outside and studying the window display. "It's Georgetown in December. There are a lot of people walking around."

"But how many of them also went into the Starbucks on Wisconsin Avenue like we did and are now at The Paper Source?"

I was impressed that Kate was so attentive to her surroundings and scolded myself for not paying more attention. I was a young woman living in a city after all. "Why would anyone be following us?" I asked. "Unless one of your dates is becoming too attentive."

"You think he's a stalker?" Kate tilted her head to one side as she thought. "Nope. None of the guys I've been seeing are that short, and I'm pretty sure none of them are whack-a-doos."

"Pretty sure?" I mumbled. "That's encouraging."

Kate shrugged. "It's DC. I can never be 100 percent sure if they're a bit unbalanced or just congressional staffers."

I couldn't see the man's face because his collar was turned up and he wore a black scarf around his neck, but he didn't seem to be moving on. I didn't know too many men who were that captivated by stationery and quirky gifts.

"Here's what we do," I said in a low voice, even though there was a hundred feet and a wall of glass between us and our potential follower. "We leave the store and walk back in the direction we came from, then duck into that alcove at the end of the block. If he stays here or walks the other way, he isn't following us."

"Sounds good," Kate said, "but we could also walk out and walk into the Sprinkles cupcake shop next door. That would be more of a win-win."

"And if he really is trailing us, he wouldn't need to move to keep an eye on us if we walk right next door," I said.

"Fine, we'll do it your way." Kate looped an arm through mine. "But once we ditch this guy, I'm coming back here to buy the Llamanoes. After I get a cupcake."

We walked out of the stationery store and made a sharp right, passing the man and taking long strides down the sidewalk. Neither of us turned to see if he was following us, but once we reached the end of the block, we hurried past the white picket fence attached to The Old Stone House and ducked through the low gate and into the gardens. I pulled Kate down low so we were crouched below the fence.

We didn't have to wait long. A minute later, the man appeared and paused at the fence, looking around. I felt my heart race, and Kate gripped my arm even tighter.

As he stepped through the gate and glanced around, I shot to my feet. "Why are you following us?"

The figure stumbled back and fell onto the ground, the thick scarf falling down to reveal bright-pink lips.

Kate leapt up beside me. "Our stalker is Leatrice?"

CHAPTER 17

"I'm not stalking you," Leatrice said once I'd helped her up. "I'm trailing after the person who *is* following you."

Kate glanced around us at the empty garden with bare tree branches and low scraggy bushes. "So you're saying someone is trailing us, and you're following that person?"

Leatrice bobbed her head up and down, the knit cap no longer hiding her distinctive Mary Tyler Moore flip. "I noticed someone loitering outside our building this morning when I did my usual security sweep of the neighborhood. I didn't think too much of it, even though I noted it in my activity log. I didn't think she was a covert agent. She didn't look the type, but you never know. The city has seen a definite uptick in sleeper spy activity."

"Yep," Kate muttered. "That sounds completely normal."

I shushed her. "Go on, Leatrice. When did you think this person started following us?"

"I heard you and Kate leave and happened to look out my window." Color crept into her cheeks, and I suspected she'd been watching us go. "Right after you headed down the street, the same woman from earlier started walking about a block behind you. Naturally, I followed."

"Naturally," Kate said. "Your disguise was pretty good, you know. We thought you were a man. I mean, a severely vertically challenged man, but still."

Leatrice beamed. "I didn't have much time to assemble my disguise. If I hadn't been in such a rush, I would have added a mustache or a wig."

"So then what happened?" I asked. "Did the woman stay behind us?"

"For a long time, yes." Leatrice looked toward the sidewalk. "But when you came out of the paper store, she walked down one of the side streets toward the canal."

"So if she dropped off, she may not have been following us," I said. "It could have been a coincidence that she was behind us."

Leatrice frowned. "I don't think so. She definitely watched you two for a while."

"That's odd," Kate said. "I've never had a woman follow me. Men, sure. That's nothing new."

"Did you recognize the woman?" I asked Leatrice. "What did she look like?"

"No, I'd never seen her before this morning." Leatrice nibbled on her heavily lipsticked lower lip. "I couldn't see much under her hat and scarf, but I could tell she was a woman from her shape."

"So we're looking for a woman-shaped woman," I said, trying to keep the exasperation out of my voice. "That narrows it down."

Kate stood up and clasped my hand. "You don't think it's one of our brides, do you?"

"Why would a bride follow us?" I asked, knowing very well that a bridezilla didn't need a logical reason to do anything.

"Who knows?" Kate threw her hands in the air. "Maybe we didn't return her phone call within the hour, maybe we weren't available for her wedding, maybe she's getting divorced and blames us."

"You're being ridiculous," I said, although I mentally reviewed our current client roster to see if anyone jumped out at me as a potential nutcase. No one sprang to mind, but that didn't give me much comfort. "Why don't we walk down the street she took and see if Leatrice recognizes her? There must be some detail that sets her apart since she followed her all over Georgetown."

"Her coat is dark green," Leatrice said. "And she's wearing boots."

"That's something," I said. "Most people in DC wear black coats, so a dark-green one shouldn't be tough to pick out of a crowd."

"So we're going to stalk the stalker?" Kate grinned. "I kind of like that."

Leatrice rubbed her hands together. "This is so exciting. What if she's a spy?"

"If she's a spy, why would she be following me and Kate?" I said, leading the way out of the small garden and back to the sidewalk.

Leatrice stopped and stared at us. "What if you're both spies?"

"We're wedding planners." Kate patted her arm. "You should know. You've crashed some of our weddings."

Leatrice didn't seem convinced. "True, but wedding planning would be the perfect cover for an international spy. Just think of all the politicians you've worked for."

"Leatrice," I said. "You know us. We're not spies."

Leatrice finally nodded and squeezed my hand. "You're right. A spy wouldn't be as messy as you are, dear."

Kate muffled a laugh behind her hand and tried to assume a serious expression. "So which way did she go?"

My elderly neighbor pointed to a side street across from us

that led down to the canal and finally to the Potomac River. "Down that street."

I pressed the button for the walk signal and watched the electric display across the street until it lit up with a green stick figure. "Let's go. There may be a chance she's still around."

Kate and Leatrice hurried after me, Leatrice jogging to keep up with my long strides and Kate taking short steps in her high-heeled boots. I waited at the intersection for them to catch up and held the collar of my coat close to my neck. Once they'd joined me, we headed down the sloped sidewalk and crossed over the canal bridge, the brown water flowing beneath us.

Kate put a hand on my arm to stop me. "There it is."

"You see a dark-green coat?" I asked, scanning the few people strolling down the street with us. "Where?"

Kate raised a finger and pointed to the pink-edged doors and windows of the shop across from us, a hot-pink old-fashioned bicycle with a flower-filled basket leaning against the lamppost out front. "You can't say no to a cupcake from Baked & Wired. They're your favorite."

She was right. The cupcakes from the Georgetown bakery and coffee shop were hands down my favorite sweet treat in the city, but I couldn't focus on buttercream at the moment. "Maybe once we locate this mystery stalker."

"I could go for a cupcake," Leatrice said. "Surveillance is hard work."

So much for my intrepid team.

Kate leaned on the bridge railing and lifted one foot to rub the instep. "Can we at least pop inside Lush and sit down for a second? These boots were not made for downhill walking."

I suppressed the urge to tell her that her shoes were never designed for any kind of walking. My eyes went to Buster and Mack's floral shop a few doors down and then scanned the rest of the street. No sign of a green coat anywhere. "Fine. But only for a minute."

Leatrice and I each took one of Kate's elbows to keep her from falling face-first on the downhill walk. I held open one side of the glass doors and let them walk in ahead of me. A bell jingled above us to announce our arrival as I was met with the distinct scent of fresh flowers and freshly brewed espresso. I would know Lush with my eyes closed.

I let the door fall behind me as I spotted a woman looking at a table set up with small potted fir trees, Jo Malone scented candles, and topiaries made out of cranberries.

Leatrice nudged me. "Dark-green coat at ten o'clock."

The woman turned at the sound of the bell and Leatrice's stage whisper and met my eyes. Well, this was a surprise.

CHAPTER 18

The woman who'd seemed so unhappy to be at the funeral protest the day before drew in her breath sharply when she spotted me. Now that I was closer to her and she wasn't bundled in a hat and scarf, I realized she was much younger than I'd originally thought. No way could she be the old guy's wife, unless he went in for child brides.

Her heart-shaped face was unlined, and there was a smattering of freckles across the bridge of her nose. The ash-brown hair that fell around her face indeed looked like it had been streaked with blond highlights at the ends, and her blue eyes blinked rapidly as she looked at me.

What was she doing here, I wondered, and why was she, of all people, following us?

Her shoulders curved forward, she lowered her head, and she shuffled toward the corner of the shop as if trying to slip out unnoticed. Luckily, my body blocked the doorway.

"I remember you," I said as she edged her way toward the door. "You were at the funeral yesterday."

Kate spun around. "What?"

I stepped in front of the woman. "You were with the protest. You were next to the man with the gray hair who seemed to be the leader."

"I'm sorry," she mumbled without meeting my eyes. "This was a mistake."

"You're one of those horrible protesters?" Kate's voice went up a couple of octaves. "Why were you following us? Did you want to get in a few more hits?"

The woman looked up at Kate's face, the purple bruise on her cheek still visible through her concealer, and flinched, shaking her head.

Mack emerged from the back of the shop wearing baby Merry in the black fabric carrier on his chest. Even though I couldn't see her head, from the direction of her flailing arms and legs I could tell the baby faced him.

"What's all the ruckus?" he asked, jiggling the baby up and down as he walked back and forth. "You woke up Merry."

The woman drew in her breath again, and her eyes fixed on Mack.

It only took a second for everything to click in my head. "You're the mother. You're the one who left the baby at the church."

The entire shop went still as every eye turned to her. Crimson flooded her cheeks, and her eyes darted around the room. I was afraid she was going to try to run through me and out the door, so I squared my body in anticipation. Instead, her shoulders sagged as if she were a puppet who'd had her strings cut, and she sank to the floor with her hands over her face.

Buster came out of the back and stood behind Mack. "What's going on?"

"I think they found the baby's mother," Mack said, his voice barely a whisper and his face crestfallen.

Buster gaped at the sobbing woman on the cement floor then

looked up at me. "How did you track her down? I thought you didn't have any leads."

"Technically we didn't find her," I said. "She was following us, although I don't know why."

"And I was following her," Leatrice added. "I thought she might be a secret agent."

Buster walked over to the woman and lifted her up by the shoulders. "Why don't you come sit down? You look like you could use a cappuccino."

"I know I could use a cappuccino," Kate said, following Buster and the woman to the long metal table near the coffee station.

Buster sat the woman on a metal stool and took the one next to her, keeping his thick arm around her shoulders. "You're among friends now. Why don't you tell us why you're here and why you left your baby at our church?"

Mack hadn't moved from where he stood near the open door to the back of the shop, but he stroked the baby's head as she fussed. The woman swiped at her eyes and pushed a strand of hair off her face and turned toward the sound of the baby's tiny cries.

"Is she okay?"

"She's fine," Mack said, holding on to the tiny pajamaed feet with his large hands and gazing down at her head. "She's an easy baby, you know."

The woman nodded. "That's good. I thought she'd find a good home if I left her with you all."

I pulled out a stool across from her. "So it's true. You're the mother." Part of me couldn't believe we'd actually located her. Or, to be more accurate, she'd located us.

She took a deep breath and straightened up. "I'm Prudence, but I like to go by Prue. My father is the leader of our church and, well . . ." She met my eyes. "You've seen what he's like."

My memories of the gray-haired man screaming curses, his

eyes blazing with hate, were fresh in my mind. "I take it he doesn't know you had a baby?"

She shook her head, her lips pressed together. "I'm only eighteen and still a senior in high school. He would kill me if he knew. My mother's been gone for a while, so it's just the two of us. He only became the way he is after she died." A pained expression passed across her face, but she gave a small shake of her head and continued. "I didn't know I was pregnant for a long time, then when I realized it I wore baggy clothes to hide the bump. He doesn't like me wearing anything tight, so it wasn't hard."

Mack took a few steps closer, and I noticed his stern expression softening.

"I'd seen you all every time we protested a funeral." Prue's eyes filled with tears. "I hated going to them, but my father made me. You and your friends always seemed so kind. I figured any people who would come out and do what you do for strangers would take good care of a baby."

"So you tracked down their church and left Merry outside?" I asked.

She nodded. "I waited around the corner to make sure someone found her. I didn't just run off." A tear snaked down her face. "I almost ran back for her, but then I saw you two come out and pick her up." She looked between Buster and Mack. "You looked so happy, I figured I'd made the right decision after all, even though it was the hardest thing I've ever done."

Buster rubbed the woman's back, then stood and moved to the large chrome coffee machine.

Mack took Buster's place, lowering himself onto the stool so the baby's feet rested on his thighs. "I'm sure she's missed you. Do you want to hold her?"

Prue looked longingly at the tiny baby, then shook her head. "I can't keep her. I don't want to get any more attached to her than I already am. It nearly killed me to walk away the first time."

"Come on." Mack lifted the sleeping child out of the front carrier, keeping one hand on the back of her head. "I've been wearing her for hours. It would give me a break."

Prue accepted the now-sleeping baby and cradled her in her arms, tracing one finger lightly down the side of Merry's face. Mack cleared his throat and looked away, blinking hard. Buster faced the coffee machine as he fiddled with the nozzles and handles, but I saw him wipe his cheeks furtively.

"Isn't there anyone else you and Merry could stay with aside from your father?" Leatrice asked, hopping onto a stool and letting her legs swing beneath her.

Prue didn't look up as she shook her head. "Everyone I know is in the church. They won't help me. They're just like my father."

Kate touched a hand to her bruise. "No, they didn't strike me as the forgiving and accepting types."

"What about the baby's father?" I asked, suspecting the answer before she gave it.

"He's my age and doesn't want to deal with a baby," the girl said. "He freaked out when I told him, and now he won't even look at me."

Kate muttered some choice words under her breath, and Mack nodded in agreement, even though I knew he normally didn't approve of cursing.

Prue choked back a sob. "Even if I got away from my father, I don't have any way to support Merry. I haven't even graduated from high school." She closed her eyes and gave a shake of her head. "What kind of life would that be for her? I want her to end up better than me."

The steam nozzle hissed as Buster finished off a pair of cappuccinos. He turned and set one in front of Prue and another in front of Kate, then turned back to the coffee station before I could get a good look at his face.

"Then why were you following us?" I asked.

She looked up. "I just wanted to make sure she was okay. I saw you two yesterday and heard you mention Merry, so I figured you knew where she was and might lead me to her. I read your T-shirts, and it was easy enough to find your business address online."

Kate looked confused for a moment, then snapped her fingers. "We both wore our Wedding Belles T-shirts."

"Not exactly the marketing we'd imagined," I said.

"I waited outside of your building for a few hours before you came out," Prue said. "I almost gave up, but then you appeared."

Leatrice bounced up and down in her stool. "That's when I saw you and thought you might be a spy."

Prue's eyes drew together in obvious confusion, but I waved a hand. "Don't mind her. She thinks everyone is a spy at some point. So you thought we'd lead you to Merry?"

She shrugged. "I hoped, although I was about to give up when you started acting weird."

"That would be when we realized Leatrice was following us," Kate said.

"I thought you'd seen me, so I went the opposite way and happened to see the Harleys outside this shop." She gazed down at her baby. "I came inside here and pretended to be looking around in hopes that Merry would be here."

"That was quite a long shot," I said. "What if she'd been somewhere else?"

Prue bit her lower lip. "I guess I would have kept coming back."

"It doesn't sound like you want to give up your baby to me," Leatrice said.

The girl took a shaky breath. "I don't have any other choice."

"Of course you do." Buster drank a shot of espresso in a single gulp and turned back around. "You and Merry can live here."

Everyone's mouths dropped open, including Mack's.

Kate glanced around the industrial-style flower shop. "Are you planning to put a cot between the flower buckets?"

Mack sat up straighter. "He means the apartment upstairs. We've been using it for storage, but it's got two bedrooms and would be the perfect size for a mother and baby."

"It's the obvious solution," Buster said. "You don't want to lose Merry and neither do we. This way you'd have someplace to live, and we'd still get to see her."

Mack nodded. "We'll watch her while you're at school."

Prue's eyes lit up, then she frowned. "An apartment in this neighborhood would be expensive, and I don't have any money." She set her mouth. "And I can't take charity."

"Who said anything about charity?" Buster asked. "We all work hard, and so can you. We need extra hands around the flower shop, especially during the holidays. We'll pay you just like we pay our other employees, and you can pay a small amount back for your room and board. But you have to finish up school before you can start working full-time."

Prue looked at both men, her eyes narrowing as she took in the hulking figures with multiple piercings wearing black leather. "But I don't know you."

Kate crossed one leg over the other, and her coat fell open to reveal plenty of bare leg. "They took care of your baby happily and with no questions asked. What more do you need to know?"

I reached a hand across the table. "I've known Buster and Mack for years, and there aren't two people I would trust more."

Kate made an indignant noise, but I ignored her.

Prue held my eyes for a moment, then looked at Buster and Mack and smiled tentatively. "Are you sure? You don't know me."

Mack shrugged. "You came back. What more do we need to know?"

Leatrice pulled a tissue out of her pocket and blew her nose.

"This is even better than busting open an international spy ring. Well, it's *as* good."

"Don't worry." Kate patted the sniffling Leatrice on the shoulder. "The day's still young."

CHAPTER 19

"Where is your wine opener?" Richard called from the kitchen over the sounds of opening and slamming drawers in rapid succession. Forget hearing the Harry Connick Jr. holiday music I had playing from my portable iPhone speaker on top of the bookshelf.

"Drawer next to the fridge," Reese called back from the stepladder where he stood wrapping white lights around the Christmas tree. He looked down at me holding a spool of string lights between my hands and dropped his voice. "I hope he's opening a bottle for himself. He definitely needs to relax."

"This is standard pre-event Richard," I said. "He won't unwind until people have tasted his food and declared it the best thing they've ever eaten."

"I thought we were keeping the food simple. Didn't you nix the three-foot snowman cheese ball and the gingerbread people made to look like each of us?"

"I think he gave up the gingerbread people only because he couldn't find a cookie cutter that looked like Hermes, but you know Richard doesn't do low-key." I inhaled the savory scents of baked Brie and the sweet and spicy nuts he'd put in the oven to warm. "Luckily, he's got holiday parties booked, and our wedding nixed all the holiday-themed food, so we're eating what he made for those. I'm just glad I'm not cooking."

Reese wisely didn't make a comment as he wrapped the end of the last string around the top of the tree and stepped down off the ladder. He stood back to admire his handiwork and wrapped an arm around my waist. "This place is starting to look pretty good."

I had to agree. My apartment—correction, our apartment now—usually erred on the side of minimalism, but the Christmas tree, pillar candles, and hanging paper stars made it look positively festive. And the combination of the fresh fir tree and Richard's cooking made it smell as good as it looked.

"That should be the last of it," Kate said as she appeared from the hallway with an armload of leftover items from our past weddings. She dumped it on the couch. "We've got a variety of cocktail napkins; striped straws in pink, gold, and lavender; and even some 'Eat, Drink, and Be Married' stir sticks."

"Perfect." I picked up a stack of cream "Heather and Jeff" napkins and fanned them out across my coffee table. "Once this party is over, I hope never to lay eyes on any of this stuff again."

"It was a great idea to have a party to use up all of this," Kate said, arranging the stir sticks and straws on the countertop between the kitchen and living room. "You know what we could have done to make it even more fun? Wear old bridesmaids' gowns." She waved a wooden stir stick at me. "Boy, do I have some doozies."

"So we'd be in awful bridesmaids' dresses and the men would be in regular clothes?" I asked. "That doesn't seem fair."

"I'll bet we could get Fern into a bridesmaids' gown." Kate wagged her eyebrows at me. "I have a burgundy velvet he'd look great in."

"Make way, make way," Richard cried as he appeared from the

kitchen holding a large tray in front of him and set it in the center of the coffee table.

Kate leaned down and breathed in. "They smell amazing. What are they?"

Richard wiped his hands off on his Santa apron. "Pepper jelly palmiers and pimento cheese puffs. But no touching until everyone gets here." He spun on his heel.

Kate pulled her hand back and frowned, shooting a look at Richard's retreating back. "Fine. Why don't I get the drinks going since someone is being such a despot with the food?"

"Don't forget we need a nonalcoholic option," I reminded her as she followed Richard into the kitchen. "Not only are Buster and Mack teetotalers, but one of our guests is only eighteen."

"I'm on it," she said.

Reese pulled me closer and brushed a strand of hair off my forehead. "I'm glad everything worked out with the baby and her mother."

"Who knew the floral business was so lucrative that Buster and Mack could own their entire building?" I gazed up at him. "What would you have done if the mother hadn't found us, and Buster and Mack had wanted to keep the baby?"

He let out a breath. "I don't know. I couldn't in good conscience have put the child into the system right before the holidays, but you also can't just keep a baby you find. I'm glad I wasn't forced into an impossible decision."

"I'm sorry I put you in another difficult situation," I said. "I seem to do that a lot."

He grinned at me. "This time it wasn't actually your fault, and there was no dead body, so it really pales in comparison to all the other times you've meddled in police investigations or the many occasions I've had to save you from a violent criminal."

I swatted at him. "You wish you needed to save me."

He pulled me closer. "I do wish you needed me to save the day more."

"I never said I didn't need you." I felt my face flush. "There are a lot of other ways I need you."

He arched an eyebrow as he lowered his head and his lips brushed over mine. I wrapped my arms around his neck and let myself sink into the kiss, feeling it all the way to my fingertips.

"Yoo hoo!" Leatrice called as she opened the door without knocking.

Reese pulled away from me and sighed. "Tomorrow I'm going out and buying a dead bolt."

I eyed Leatrice as she walked into the room, the eight blue-and-white candles on her headband bobbing as she set a round tray down next to Richard's hot hors d'oeuvres display. She wore her brightly colored Christmas tree skirt with the plug dangling from the back and a red sweatshirt.

"Better get two just to be safe," I said.

Hermes, who she'd been watching while we prepared for the party, scampered in with her, jumping onto the couch and yipping happily as he ran from one end to the other.

Sidney Allen came in behind the small Yorkie, holding a foil-topped bottle in a shimmering red velveteen bag and two small wrapped presents. He wore a dark suit, like he did at every event, and the pants were hiked up high on his chest so the belt appeared to be nearly looped around his armpits. For once, he wasn't wearing the headset I was so used to seeing him scream into as he coordinated his performers.

"Glad you could make it," I said, taking the bottle from him. "We aren't quite ready, but we're getting there." I pointed to the tree in the corner. "Grab bag gifts go under there."

Leatrice waved a hand at me. "The only reason we're early is I wanted to get a good place for my pigs-in-a-blanket wreath."

I peered down at the circle of hotdogs wrapped in golden-brown pastry. With the bow at the bottom cut out of strips of red peppers, it did indeed look like a wreath. It smelled, however, like a plate of hotdogs. I couldn't wait until Richard saw it sitting beside his delicately shaped palmiers and cheese puffs dusted with finely grated parmesan.

Reese rubbed his hands together. "Now we're talking."

Richard came out of the kitchen holding the baked Brie topped with cherry compote and stopped dead in his tracks when he spotted Leatrice. He inhaled sharply when his eyes dropped to the hot dog wreath. "What in the name of—?"

"It's a pigs-in-a-blanket wreath," I said before he could make a snarky comment. "Isn't it clever?"

Hermes leapt off the couch, ran to Richard, sniffed his leg, then ran back to the couch. Richard's frozen expression didn't change as he nodded, setting the baked Brie on the counter between the living room and kitchen.

He came up behind me, giving Hermes a pat, and whispered, "What's on her head?"

"Interesting hat, Leatrice," I said. "Where did you get it?"

"Holiday sale last year at Filene's." Leatrice reached up and touched the stuffed fabric candles. "You don't see many Christmas hats with candles, do you?"

"That's because it's a menorah," Richard muttered.

"Who wants some bubbly?" Kate asked as she came out of the kitchen holding a tray of champagne flutes with cranberries floating on top.

"Yes, please." Fern walked through the open door taking small steps and barely moving anything above his knees. His crimson suit was skintight with gold piping along the edges, and he wore a snowy-white ascot with a jeweled star at his neck, making him look very much like a slimmed-down version of Santa Claus. A green-and-red gift bag hung from one wrist. "I had to walk two blocks. This suit is barely made for standing, much less walking distances."

"I wouldn't call two blocks a distance," I said, taking the gift bag from him since he clearly couldn't lift his arm to hand it to me.

"You would if you were trying to fit into your skinny suit." He let out a tiny breath, straining the one gold button on his jacket. "I hope you have some keto diet food."

I didn't even know what foods counted as keto, but I felt sure that anything Richard had made contained enough butter, cheese, and real cream to float a barge. "You're starting a diet *before* the holidays?"

Fern glanced at the trays of food and looked pained, either from the suit cutting off his circulation or the fact that he couldn't eat anything.

"Do like I do, and go on a liquid diet." Kate handed him a champagne flute and popped a gold-striped straw in it so he barely had to raise his arm to drink.

"Good thinking." Fern drained the glass in a single sip. "I feel thinner already."

I didn't have the heart to tell either of them that a liquid diet did not mean drinking only booze.

Fern scanned the group, his eyes settling on Leatrice, and he shuffled over to her. "Sweetie, did you know your skirt has a plug hanging from the back?"

"It lights up," she said, pointing to the tiny lights embedded in the fabric. "But it's not very practical. You have to stand right next to an outlet and not move a lot."

Only Leatrice would be undeterred by a plug dangling from her clothing.

Richard motioned to our tree. "Don't you actually need a Christmas tree skirt? I say we plug her in and lay her down under there."

I elbowed him. "Be nice. It's a holiday party."

"I'm always nice, darling." He gave Reese a simpering smile. "Right, Detective?"

Reese nodded a little too eagerly as Richard left us to return to the kitchen. "I think I liked it better when Richard ignored me."

"Too late," I said. "There's no going back now."

He laughed and entwined his fingers with mine. "Good."

I felt a flutter in my stomach and picked up a glass of champagne. I was still getting used to the idea of having a boyfriend, not to mention a hot one, and much less a live-in one. Sometimes I felt like pinching myself to make sure it was real.

"Look who we found on our way up," Mack said, walking in with baby Merry strapped to his chest and Buster and Prue both carrying armfuls of colorful boxes. Mack swept an arm behind him to reveal a tall, broad-shouldered man with dark hair flecked with gray at the temples.

"Daniel!" Kate nearly dropped the tray of glasses when she saw Reese's older brother.

"I take it you didn't warn her he was coming?" Reese asked me.

I shook my head. "I was afraid of what she'd wear if she thought there were going to be any eligible men here."

As it was, her white angora sweater left little to the imagination.

Kate set the tray down without spilling anything and hurried over to Daniel Reese. "I had no idea you were coming." She glanced over her shoulder and narrowed her eyes at me.

Daniel smiled, looking very much like his brother. "I wouldn't miss it."

"Come on in, everyone," I said, ignoring Kate's pointed look and waving everyone inside. "Presents for the gift exchange go under the tree."

I turned up the volume on the holiday jazz as Leatrice began walking around the room holding the tray with her hotdog wreath, the plug to her skirt bouncing around her legs. Richard passed glasses of booze-free punch over the counter, and I noticed Prue smile as she took one of Leatrice's pigs-in-a-blanket. Mack bounced the baby gently on his chest in time to "Deck the Halls", which she seemed to be sleeping through, and Buster produced several boxes of glass ball ornaments I recognized as one of the holiday items they sold in their shop.

Buster winked at me. "You did say the theme was leftover inventory purge, right?"

"Your leftover inventory is a lot fancier than mine," I told him as I eyed the blown-glass orbs.

Fern stutter-stepped over to me. "Baby-mama is cute." He angled his head as he stared at her across the room. "And young. You don't think she'll let me fix her hair, do you? I haven't worked on anyone young in forever."

I leveled my gaze at him, and he gave a nervous laugh. "Aside from you and Kate, of course. You know I don't mean that you two are old, sweetie."

"Thanks," I said.

"Don't mention it." He patted my arm and began making his way geisha girl-style to Prue.

I made a mental note to warn the girl not to give Fern free rein with her hair unless she wanted to end up with a transformation worthy of the witness relocation program.

I saw the door open and our cake baker friend, Alexandra, poke her head inside. I waved her in and tried not to stare when I saw whose hand she was holding as she pulled him behind her. "Is that the detective you worked with on our last case?" I asked Reese.

The mousy-haired man with the questionable combover smiled and nodded to us before turning his attention back to the tall glamorous woman next to him. He looked as shocked to be holding her hand as I was, although I'd thought they'd looked like

LAURA DURHAM

they were getting cozy during the police investigation we'd met him on.

"It sure is," Reese said, shaking his head. "Doesn't Alexandra live in Scotland?"

"Yep," I said, watching the baker flip her long brown hair off her shoulder and set a pink bakery box on the coffee table. "She flies over to do our high-profile cakes a few times a year."

Reese pointed to the box. "Do you think she brought cake?"

"The oddest couple of the century just walked in and you're thinking about cake?" I asked him, secretly hoping Alexandra had brought some of her famous sweets as well.

He looped an arm around me and pulled me close. "Cake isn't all I'm thinking about."

I felt myself blush and looked around to see if anyone had heard. The nearest person was Buster who was unpacking ornaments and handing them out for people to hang.

Reese took a red-and-green-swirled glass ball and passed it to me. "Here, babe."

As I took the ornament from him and hung it on our first Christmas tree together, I felt happier than I had in a long time. Even knowing I had a wedding in a couple of days with a bride who rivaled the Grinch couldn't put a damper on the feeling of home I got as I looked around the room. Richard had left the kitchen and removed his apron, and he stood next to the couch petting Hermes on the head. He looked calmer than usual, and I felt surprised he wasn't scurrying around after Leatrice trying to get people to eat his hors d'oeuvres instead. Maybe he really was over the disappointment of being left off the list, although somehow I doubted it.

"Cheers to surviving another year," Kate said from her perch on Daniel's lap as she raised a glass of champagne. "Together."

Everyone raised their glasses and clinked them.

Reese locked eyes with me, his hazel eyes deepening to green. "I'll drink to that."

THE END

SINCE IT'S THE HOLIDAYS, Richard has decided to share a couple of his party recipes on the next pages (most of them borrowed and adapted from *Southern Living*, which he loves and reads from cover to cover). Enjoy!

Missed a book in the series? Check out the entire series listed in order after the recipes!

Want to read another novella—for free? Flip one more page, and sign up to my VIP Reader List and get a free novella (book #3)!

Wishing you the happiest of holidays!

PEPPER JELLY PALMIERS

1 (17.3-oz.) package frozen puff pastry sheets, thawed
1 and 1/4 cup finely shredded Parmesan cheese
6 tablespoons chopped fresh chives
1/2 teaspoon kosher salt
1/2 teaspoon black pepper
2/3 cup hot pepper jelly
Parchment paper

Step 1
Roll 1 pastry sheet into a 12- x 10-inch rectangle on lightly floured surface. Sprinkle with half of cheese, 3 Tbsp. chives, and 1/4 tsp. each salt and pepper. Roll up pastry, jelly-roll fashion, starting with each short side and ending at middle of pastry sheet. Wrap pastry tightly with parchment paper. Repeat procedure with remaining pastry sheet, cheese, chives, salt, and pepper. Freeze for1 to 24 hours.

Step 2
Preheat oven to 375°. Line baking sheets with parchment paper. Remove pastries from freezer, and let stand at room temperature for 10 minutes. Cut each roll into 1/4-inch-thick slices, and place on baking sheets.

Step 3
Bake, in batches, 20 minutes or until golden.

Step 4
Microwave pepper jelly in a microwave-safe bowl on HIGH for 1 minute. Brush 1/2 tsp. pepper jelly onto each palmier. Serve immediately.

Make Ahead: Prepare Step 1 of the recipe, and wrap the dough in plastic wrap. Freeze up to 1 month. Resume with Step 2 about an hour before serving.

CHERRY WALNUT BRIE

1/3 cup cherry preserves
1 tablespoon balsamic vinegar
1/8 teaspoon freshly ground pepper
1/8 teaspoon salt
1 (8-oz.) Brie round, rind removed from top
Chopped toasted walnuts

Stir together cherry preserves, balsamic vinegar, pepper, and salt in a bowl. Drizzle over warm Brie round. Top with walnuts. Serve with crackers.

ALSO BY LAURA DURHAM

Read the entire Annabelle Archer Series in order:

Better Off Wed

For Better Or Hearse

Dead Ringer

Review To A Kill

Death On The Aisle

Night of the Living Wed

Eat, Prey, Love

Groomed For Murder

Wed or Alive

To Love and To Perish

Marry & Bright

To get notices whenever I release a new book, follow me on BookBub:

https://www.bookbub.com/profile/laura-durham

LEAVE A REVIEW

Did you enjoy this book? You can make a big difference!

I'm extremely lucky to have a loyal bunch of readers, and honest reviews are the best way to help bring my books to the attention of new readers.

If you enjoyed *Marry and Bright*, I would be forever grateful if you could spend two minutes leaving a review (it can be as short as you like) on Goodreads, Bookbub, or your favorite retailer.

Thanks for reading and reviewing!

ACKNOWLEDGMENTS

As always, an enormous thank you to all of my wonderful readers, especially my beta readers and my review team. I never give you enough time, but you always come through for me. A special shout-out to the beta readers who caught all my goofs this time: Linda Fore, Tony Noice, Sheila Kraemer, Wendy Green, Carol Spayde, Katherine Munro, and Tricia Knox. Thank you!!

A heartfelt thank you to everyone who leaves reviews. They really make a difference, and I am grateful for every one of them!

I learned a lot about Christian biker gangs for this book and was very impressed by them. One of the themes I revisit often in my books is looking beyond appearances, and I think this fits perfectly with these tough guys (and ladies) with hearts of gold.

ABOUT THE AUTHOR

Laura Durham has been writing for as long as she can remember and has been plotting murders since she began planning weddings over twenty years ago in Washington, DC. Her first novel, BETTER OFF WED, won the Agatha Award for Best First Novel.

When she isn't writing or wrangling brides, Laura loves traveling with her family, standup paddling, perfecting the perfect brownie recipe, and reading obsessively.

She loves hearing from readers and she would love to hear from you! Send an email or connect on Facebook, Instagram, or Twitter (click the icons below).

Find me on:
www.lauradurham.com
laura@lauradurham.com

facebook.com/authorlauradurham
twitter.com/reallauradurham
instagram.com/lauradurhamauthor

CPSIA information can be obtained
at www.ICGtesting.com
Printed in the USA
LVHW041922120120
643360LV00004B/537/P

9 781949 496000